Isaac Al

ALSO BY THE AUTHOR

POETRY

Poems
Poems, Book Two

FICTION

Stories
The Calling

ACKNOWLEDGEMENTS

I'd like to thank David Restaino for his help in editing the manuscript.

I'd like to thank Mark Swan for the brilliant cover illustration.

I'd like to thank Hashem for all His inspiration.

And I'd like to thank the reader for choosing to pick up this book!

Copyright © Joseph Estevez 5784 / 2023

All rights reserved. No part of this book may be reproduced or used in any manner without written permission of the copyright owner except for the use of quotations in a book review.

ISBN: 9798862048629

'...the prose, though simple and straightforward, is more than competent, and engaging in its own way. I certainly found myself more invested in the story and the characters than I expected'

– James Kinsley, reviewer on *Isaac Abrams*

ISAAC

ABRAMS

Joseph Estevez

PART I

CHAPTER I

Mr and Mrs Abrams were preparing the living room for the reception of their son, who had been studying at yeshiva in Israel. They were aided by their other three children, Mordechai, Sarah, and Ruth. Decorations spelling 'Welcome Home' arched under the ceiling, and blue and white balloons occupied every corner. A meal had been prepared. The smell of potatoes and meat filled the room. Servings of boiled potatoes and meatloaf were placed on the dining table accompanied by several side dishes. Soon enough, the table was set and ready for the participants.

One by one, Eliezer Blume, Simon Gold, and Ariel Silver arrived. Mrs Abrams had invited her son's friends to participate in the reception to maximise the joy of their son upon his return home. Mr Abrams kindly reminded them to put on a kippah. They would have to wear one whilst partaking in the meal, and there were plenty of extra kippot in the house (they had not brought one with them).

After donning kippot that Mr Abrams had provided them, the friends stood around; Simon's eyes glanced at the meal, and Eliezer couldn't be still amidst the delicious scents. After enough waiting, Mrs Abrams returned the meatloaf and boiled potatoes to the kitchen to keep warm.

Mr and Mrs Abrams wondered what was taking their son so long to return home. They called him, but he didn't pick up the phone. Eliezer, Simon, and Ariel conversed in order to distract themselves from their worry regarding their friend's delay. Mr and Mrs Abrams's children did the same.

At around half past six, after flight delays and a taxi from Heathrow Airport to Golders Green, Isaac opened the front door and, carrying a stuffed backpack and carry-on, rolled his large suitcase through the entrance. With the sight of the interior of his quiet home, which granted privacy from the outside world, he was overcome by emotion, both by the comfortable, familiar feeling of being home again and by yearning to remain in the land of Israel to be with his friends and classmates and to be learning. He felt a contraction in his chest, a tightness in his throat, and, amidst pulling all this weight, was on the verge of tears.

He entered the living room and was met with a flood of cheers from his family and close friends. He grinned upon seeing them, quickly forgetting whatever melancholic thoughts he had had. Mordechai, his older brother, threw his arms around him – indeed, no other person showed him as much affection as he did – and the other members of his family and friends also embraced him. Mordechai and Mr Abrams took his belongings to his bedroom as Mrs Abrams and her two daughters brought out the hot dishes, and they all sat down to eat what had been intended to be a late lunch but turned out to be a dinner.

Isaac's family and friends bombarded him with questions about Israel and yeshiva. The Abrams had gone to Israel once several years ago and, apart from Ariel's visit to see relatives there five years prior, that represented the totality of the diners' experience travelling there.

After the meal, Isaac's family left him to be with his friends on the sofa (they would have ample opportunity to enquire further about his experiences later), and he was overcome with joy to be reunited with the three of them again. He sat at the end of the sofa, which gave him a full view of his three friends' faces.

'How's The Team doing?' asked Isaac.

'The Team' was a name the four of them had given themselves as a group after having formed such a strong bond whilst attending secondary school during their time at yeshiva together.

'Good,' said Simon. 'I actually had a good run this past summer. I didn't tell you, but I got a pretty good role in a play, and the show ran for two months at the theatre.'

'Wow,' said Isaac, delighted to hear that his time at the Royal Academy of Dramatic Art had been followed by such success. 'So, I'm guessing you were able to do shows outside of Shabbat?'

'No,' said Simon, 'I knew beforehand that it would be on Friday and Saturday nights, but… it was such a prominent position, and I really wanted it. I thought, I can't just let this opportunity pass.'

Isaac only stared at his friend. He was able to maintain a smile on his face – how could he not? Apart from smiling out of politeness, he had not seen his friends for three years. He had visited home a handful of times during his studying in Israel, but Ariel had been away studying mathematics at Oxford, Simon had been consumed by his studying acting at the Academy, whilst Eliezer had been busy at work or on holiday somewhere. Inside, he was crumbling in deep sadness and despair. How could his good friend have been violating Shabbat? Had he comprehended the gravity of his intended actions? Eliezer was the next to speak, and Isaac eagerly welcomed this, hoping for relief.

'I've been working at the fitness centre,' said Eliezer, who worked as a personal trainer. 'It's been going great. I've been making a lot of progress with my team. We've been doing a lot of research on health and using it with our clients and promoting ourselves on social media. We're really getting our name out there and we're starting to experience a lot of success.'

'OK, great,' said Isaac, nodding. Though the others were quick to voice their support for him, something about Eliezer's words and the way he related them to them made Isaac feel a little insecure. 'Do you find time to study?'

'Sure. We dedicate a lot of time doing research throughout the week.'

'I was thinking more along the lines of Torah.'

Eliezer paused, looking a bit taken aback.

'Oh. Er..., no, not really.'

Simon laughed. 'When was the last time you've been to synagogue, even?'

Eliezer blushed.

Isaac saw that Ariel was blushing, too.

'And you, Ari, how have you been?' asked Isaac.

'I've been great. I got accepted into the actuary sciences programme at the University of London.'

'Mazal tov,' said Isaac. This was the only response that seemed to merit this phrase out of all the mentions of personal achievements.

'Thank you.'

'Wow,' said Simon, looking at Eliezer to his right and Ariel to his left. 'It's so great to see you guys again.'

'You guys haven't seen each other this whole time?' asked Isaac.

Ariel shook his head.

'I was at Oxford.'

'Wow,' said Eliezer, 'The Team is back once again!'

Mr and Mrs Abrams started putting the dirty plates away. Simon got up and asked, 'Should we help you?'

'No, we've got it,' said Mrs Abrams. 'Thank you, though.'

'We should hang out sometime soon,' said Isaac as the rest of them got up from the sofa. 'Ari, you shall be in London now, so it should be easier.'

'Right,' said Ariel.

'Yes, we should!' agreed Simon.

'I'm on board,' said Eliezer.

'Great,' said Isaac.

Eliezer, Simon, and Ariel returned the kippot to Mr Abrams and thanked him for letting them use them.

'You're very welcome,' said Mr Abrams, who walked them out.

Isaac, watching in horror, trailed behind them as he witnessed his best friends walk without any head covering to the front door.

'You're welcome anytime,' Mr Abrams assured them as they waved goodbye at him and Isaac.

Isaac waved back as his jaw hung.

They descended the front steps, and Mr Abrams closed the front door.

Isaac returned to the living room, taking it all in. His strength gave way, and he sat on the sofa, staring absent-mindedly ahead as Mr and Mrs Abrams returned the empty bottles and glasses to the kitchen. What on earth had happened to his friends? And what little he did know – Simon violating Shabbat; Eliezer not going to synagogue! How could they have allowed themselves to get to such a degraded state?

'Isaac,' called Mr Abrams, collecting a pair of wine glasses, 'I know you're probably tired from your travels, but could you help us out just a bit?'

'Sure,' said Isaac, jumping off the sofa to help his parents clean the dining table.

After clearing the table, Isaac said to his father, 'Could I talk to you for a moment?'

'Sure,' said Mr Abrams.

They sat beside each other on the sofa.

'What's up?'

'I can't believe it. It seems like Eliezer, Simon, and Ari are becoming less observant. I fear that they're no longer frum.' Isaac was heartbroken as he uttered these words.

'Right. I had never seen them without their kippot before. I had requested that they put one on prior to eating.'

A wave of silence swept across the room. Isaac stared absent-mindedly past his father. He sulked. He felt powerless.

'How could they do this?'

Mr Abrams took in a deep breath, choosing carefully the right words with which to console his son.

'I don't know. It seems none of us do, but I would suggest that you not be so quick to judge. You simply don't know what they're going through – what circumstances, family pressures, personal struggles.'

'But they're going through so much success,' argued Isaac, then correcting himself, 'career success. Ari got into graduate school, I presume Eliezer's making money, and Simon just did a play.'

'Right, but,' started Mr Abrams, 'still…, you should give them the benefit of the doubt, until you know the full picture – or at least, you shouldn't really judge others until you're in their place.'

There was a bit more discussion related to this topic before Mr Abrams suggested that Isaac was stressed after his long trip home or from jetlag. Isaac only wished this were the case, but upon retiring to his dim bedroom, he could not think of anything else but his friends. What circumstances *were* they going through? He was curious.

CHAPTER II

Isaac arose the next morning and hurried to make the morning service on time at his synagogue. After shacharit was over, the congregants of his synagogue, young and old, flooded him with more questions and welcomes. He confirmed with several congregants that he had no intention of leaving London for the time being, that he had no idea what his next step would be, and that he very much enjoyed his time in Israel. It took roughly an extra fifteen minutes to leave the synagogue due to everyone's questions.

Soon after returning home, he was the only one left there as it was Monday, and everyone was off to work or engaging in their other endeavours. He finally had some peace, quiet, and privacy. He sat on his bed, and he finally unleashed the emotions he had repressed for almost a full day now. He sobbed, wetting the palms of his hands with tears. He kept thinking about Israel, about the wonderful time and memories he had made at Yeshivat Shalom. It was truly a special programme with special people. What he would have done to go back in time, to spend one more week there. The programme ended after Tisha B'Av, but he chose to stay for a little longer to engage in other learning opportunities and spiritual experiences. He would've been perfectly happy to stay there and learn forever. He could've stayed longer. Why hadn't he stayed there another week? He had felt guilty about delaying his visiting his family, but he would've come back eventually anyway. He missed Israel – the pleasant weather, the people, the spiritual growth – and now he was here. He wasn't sure if this was the right place for him to be or remain. He stared absent-mindedly at his desk in front of him, his vision blurred with the tears.

He wiped his tears with the back of his hands. He wasn't at yeshiva anymore, but he wanted to recreate the experience he had had there here, a continuation of sorts.

So, he spent that whole day learning the Gemara tractate on Shabbos. He passed the next two days studying Torah and socialising with his family after everyone had come home in the evening. He studied for several hours straight with the only interruption being a half-hour lunch break. It helped that his family was gone for most of the day. He was starting to feel relief from his remorse, and soon enough, it had evolved into a feeling of passion and excitement.

On Wednesday, in the late afternoon, Isaac was studying the weekly Parashah when Mrs Abrams knocked on the open wooden door in his bedroom.

'Excuse me,' she said.

Isaac looked up from the open Chumash.

'I wanted to ask you,' she said, 'what are your plans next?'

Mrs Abrams was a short, thin woman with long, dark hair and a gentle voice.

Isaac thought about it. 'I don't know.' He sulked. He knew that studying forever in Israel was not a possibility.

'So, you don't know whether you want to work or go to school?'

Isaac knew he could go to university, but what would he study? He could think of nothing that interested him outside of

Torah, and he could not see himself employed in a profession and enjoying it.

'No, I don't know.'

'All right, well, you're going to have to choose something eventually, Isaac. You don't need to rush; I wouldn't want you going into something and hating it, but you should really start thinking about what it is you want to do in life.'

Isaac knew what he wanted to do in life. He just had to find out what occupation he could tolerate the most. He nodded. 'OK.'

Mrs Abrams nodded and smiled. Then, she left, her footsteps sounding on the wooden floor in the corridor as she returned to the living room.

Isaac looked at the text in front of him, but he wasn't reading it. He was now faced with the extraordinary pressure of deciding what career he would like to commit to for the rest of his life. He couldn't have predicted such misery upon his return to England. He had thought he would've been happier upon returning home. It was like he had left something important behind at his yeshiva dormitory, but he had brought all of his material things. Little had he known that the best days of his life were now behind him, and ahead of him was grey.

He then thought of his friends and his encounter with them last night and, though perhaps equal in arousing hopelessness within him, it provided a desirable distraction to him as he no longer had to meditate on his own struggles, but on the shortcomings of others.

He could not let go of the sight of his friends handing the kippot to his father. He was utterly heartbroken. He was starting to feel a little bit of regret. Had he messed up by staying an extra year? After passing his A Levels with high marks, rather than go to university, he had decided to go to yeshiva for two years to strengthen his foundation of Torah before studying to work. He had then asked his parents whether he could stay a third year, to which they agreed, though it would be the last one for which they would pay. What were his friends up to during this time? Maybe, had he come back after the second year at yeshiva, he could have prevented their suddenly becoming less observant. He could've been here to encourage them to do the mitzvot and correct them had they done something wrong and overall support them, but he checked himself. Those three years of study were absolutely necessary for his spiritual growth. How could he know for sure whether choosing to stay would have prevented their becoming less religious?

So, what was he to do? How was he to bring them back to a religious life? He came up with a list of ideas. After twenty minutes of writing, he studied his entries and concluded that the ideas were too aggressive.

Something happened during those three years, some circumstance that caused each of them to turn away from Judaism. He was determined to find out what it was and then correct it.

CHAPTER III

Isaac suggested that he, Eliezer, Simon, and Ariel go out for pizza the next day, and they all agreed. Seeing that they had not seen each other during his time in Israel until his return, he assumed he was the nucleus of The Team.

The jetlag had worn off, and Isaac enjoyed seeing his neighbours and the members of his community again. He quite enjoyed the time he spent learning at home.

Thursday afternoon was cloudy, though it wasn't forecast to rain. At two o'clock, the members of The Team met outside the front doors of Chaim's Pizza. Eliezer, Simon, and Ariel were all wearing their kippot, and Isaac assumed that maybe it was because they were going out to eat or because, whilst inside, they wouldn't want the other community members catching sight of them without one.

They entered the pizzeria, which smelled of baked bread and cheese, joined the queue, and after placing their orders, Ariel found them a table in the lower level towards the back. Isaac, Eliezer, and Simon carried their trays there. It wasn't so crowded at the time, with some groups here and there, and no one was close enough to hear their conversation.

Isaac thought not to bring up the subject of their observance – or lack thereof – immediately, so he let Eliezer speak about his excitement over the success of his work. Simon reiterated his excitement over Ariel's admission to the University of London, for which Eliezer and Isaac praised him as well.

'How's auditioning?' asked Eliezer, who sat opposite Isaac, before taking a bite of his Margherita pizza.

Simon sighed. 'I haven't really been offered anything; I should probably talk to my agent.'

'You have an agent?' asked Isaac.

'Yeah, can you believe it?' He sat diagonally opposite Isaac. He braced himself on his elbow against the surface of the table having long consumed his slice of pizza. 'I got one shortly before my graduation. She was the one who helped me get the role in the play I was in. Thing is, I haven't been able to get anything since. I've been going to auditions, but no response.'

'You shall get one soon,' said Eliezer.

'Yeah, you're very talented,' said Isaac.

Simon smiled. 'Thanks.'

Isaac had seen Simon act in various roles in plays whilst at yeshiva during secondary school, and the Royal Academy of Dramatic Art was certainly not an easy school to get into.

'How's your sister?' asked Ariel. Simon's sister was up in Scotland studying at the University of St Andrews.

'Oh, she's great,' said Simon, 'loving it there.'

There was a brief moment of silence. Ariel, who sat to Isaac's right, stared ahead with his hands folded and his elbows over the table. There was a television screen to Isaac's right showing a news report at a low volume. Isaac was the only one left still eating. He thought that now would be a good time to bring up the subject of religion.

'Do you guys still consider yourselves religious?' asked Isaac.

They all stopped to think.

'I don't think so,' said Eliezer.

'Not as much, that's for sure,' said Ariel.

'I still keep Shabbat and other things whilst I'm at home,' said Simon, 'but apart from that, not really.'

Isaac felt his spirit sink. 'Well, why not? What happened?'

Ariel stared at Eliezer, thinking he would speak first, but Eliezer's eyes were downcast. Simon scratched his curly brown hair, shuffling in his seat, and smiling anxiously. It was like they were on trial.

Maybe this wasn't the right time to talk about it, thought Isaac. Maybe he should've asked them in private when they were one-on-one.

'This is kind of embarrassing, but it started for me shortly after starting school,' said Simon.

'Same here,' Ariel said quickly in his support. 'Shortly after starting Oxford, I quickly became less religious.'

Isaac was a bit upset that Ariel was trying to defend Simon. It was like he was trying to validate his lifestyle.

'There are just so many distractions,' said Simon.

'It's a lot,' said Ariel. 'It was very difficult with schoolwork and other responsibilities.'

'But what specifically distracted you?' Isaac asked Simon.

'I guess with classes, working on things with people, I just didn't have the time, and it just became sort of easier to just,' said Simon, 'do my own thing, I guess. I still keep kosher when I'm out, though.'

'I don't know,' said Eliezer. 'I honestly became less religious when we were still in yeshiva, even. My parents were upset about that, but I guess I was preparing them for what was to come. I dropped everything once we were done with yeshiva. This is actually my first Jewish experience since then – apart from going to your house last Sunday, Isaac. I didn't do so well in school; not my thing. I admire how you got out and studied in Israel, Isaac. I couldn't have done that.'

These words relating their lack of observance mixed with the praise at the very end felt like fire and ice in Isaac's bones. He was also shocked that Eliezer would relate his becoming less observant with his poor experience at yeshiva.

He felt he should stop his interrogation here. There was an obvious indifference, and, as they could not pinpoint an exact event that discouraged their spirituality, he was left with the conclusion that it was a result of their environment or lack of capabilities.

They spoke of their memories whilst at yeshiva, which was delightful to Isaac, but the current state of his friends made the delight not last long. They recited their graces after meal, put their trays away, and headed out the door. Isaac walked after them and, whilst looking absent-mindedly at their backs, felt a strong sense of nostalgia tinged with the melancholic feeling that it had long been the end of an era. He caught up eventually to walk beside them on the pavement. Walking through the streets of North London, they engaged in conversation, pointing out sites of their memories during their adolescence as they passed them by, and after a couple of streets, Eliezer, Simon, and Ariel removed their kippot from their heads as they ambled. Isaac felt as though he no longer recognised them. This trend endured after each separated from the group until Isaac was left alone on his way back home.

CHAPTER IV

Isaac could not help but ruminate on the revelations mentioned during lunch that day along the way home. How was he to make his friends observant again?

He walked through a narrow path that separated his house from the next, dodging the puddles from the rain from earlier that week.

Upon reaching the end of the path, just before he could turn left, he caught sight of Thomas Bannister, his next-door neighbour, exiting Mr Bannister's car.

'Isaac!' cried Thomas, who ran up to him and embraced him.

Isaac grinned whilst being embraced.

Thomas was twenty-one years old, like Isaac. He was slightly taller, thin, and with dark hair that was stark against his pale complexion. This was in slight contrast to Isaac, whose face was still a bit red from having lived in the Middle East for three years.

Isaac was happy to meet Thomas. They used to play games together in each other's gardens, especially during the summer, throughout their childhoods. As Isaac had gone to Jewish day school and Thomas attended a state school (the Bannisters weren't Jewish), their get-togethers had become rarer, though their friendliness had always prevailed and, upon having formed their own social circles at secondary school, their engagements had ceased. What Thomas had been up to, Isaac did not know, and he couldn't remember the last time he had seen him, though this proved to be a certain delight.

'How have you been?' asked Thomas.

'Great,' said Isaac.

Mr Bannister got out of the car and waved at Isaac as he circled around behind it and said hello, and Isaac did the same.

'How have you been?' asked Isaac.

'Great!' said Thomas, having just pulled out a suitcase from the boot. 'I just got back from travelling in Iceland with some uni friends. It was amazing!'

One would have thought that the sun was shining by the joyous expression on Thomas's face and the happiness that exuded from his green eyes, but the grey clouds had no intention of parting any time soon.

'Wow, so glad to hear,' said Isaac. 'So, you went to uni?'

'Yes, I went to Cambridge, where I studied history. I graduated just this year.'

'Congratulations,' said Isaac. 'So, what are your plans now?'

Thomas shrugged. 'Don't know; still trying to figure it out.'

'Well, that certainly makes two of us.'

Isaac saw that George, his older brother, was carrying a large bag up the front steps to Thomas's house. He smiled at Isaac in acknowledgement, and Isaac smiled back and waved.

'Can I help you carry anything?'

'No, thanks,' said Thomas, lifting his suitcase in his right hand to show. 'This is it. So, what have you been up to? I haven't been around much to see you since I've been at Cambridge.'

And Isaac, to quench any guilt on his part, said, 'I've been in Israel studying at yeshiva.'

Thomas gasped, his jaw hanging and his eyes wide open.

'No way!'

And Isaac, whose countenance was mild, swallowed.

'Amazing! How was Israel?'

'Amazing,' agreed Isaac.

'So, what do you do in yeshiva? What did you study?'

Isaac didn't want to burden Thomas with words foreign to him, so he summarised, 'A collection of books called Gemara that explains the details of Jewish oral law and mussar, which is basically about improving one's character traits.'

'Fascinating!' responded Thomas.

Despite the sudden nostalgia due to thinking about Israel, Isaac couldn't help but notice that the intense awe on Thomas's face was ever-present throughout the conversation. How he wished that his friends would have the same enthusiasm, but it brought him much pleasure to see in Thomas the amount of enthusiasm he had felt whilst in Israel. He was also starting to wonder whether something about the air of Iceland made its consumers permanently happy.

'Yeah,' said Isaac, nodding as he bit his lip and looked down.

'So, there is an oral law in Judaism?

'That was passed down from Mount Sinai,' said Isaac casually.

'Amazing. And what does the oral law describe?'

Isaac couldn't believe he was having an in-depth conversation about Judaism with his non-Jewish friend. Their conversations tended to revolve around other subjects when they used to speak more often.

'A lot of things. It describes the ways a Jew can observe the mitzvot.'

'The commandments,' interpreted Thomas.

'Correct.'

'Wow,' said Thomas, his brow raised. 'It's great to see you. We should definitely hang out sometime.'

'Sure,' said Isaac, enjoying the idea. Thomas and his family always portrayed good manners and behaviour.

Thomas rolled his suitcase around on the pavement. 'I'm actually going to visit my sister in York for a couple of weeks. George is coming with me.'

'What about your parents?'

'They've got work,' said Thomas, 'but when I come back, I'd really love to get together.'

'I look forward to it. Please give Emily my regards.'

They waved goodbye to each other.

That was the first time that day that Isaac portrayed a genuine smile. He ascended the front steps of his terraced house, pleased by the conversation and reunion he had with his old friend and good neighbour. Hopefully, they would be able to socialise much in the future. Such exciting prospects dispelled the worries with which Isaac's head had been previously buzzing, whatever they had been.

CHAPTER V

Shabbat was coming. It was Isaac's first Shabbat since he had returned to London. Though he still ruminated on his cherished moments of Israel, the sadness was gone with the catharsis brought by the many tears he had shed that week, and he was now perfectly content to be back home in the United Kingdom. Mr and Mrs Abrams were preparing the house for Shabbat. Their four children aided them.

Everyone was dressed in their favourite clothes in honour of Shabbat. Sarah and Ruth did the shopping. Along the way they talked about school, their friends, and their teachers and shared things they had learnt at school that week. Mrs Abrams was in the kitchen preparing Israeli salad. Mordechai was upstairs in his bedroom catching up with friends over the telephone and wishing them Shabbat Shalom. Mr Abrams was on the living room sofa reading the weekly Torah portion. Isaac, dressed in his black Shabbat suit and wearing a turquoise tie, was doing the same in his bedroom. The pre-Shabbat atmosphere of the household was full of excitement for the coming of Shabbat, but already quiet and peaceful as everyone concentrated on their tasks. Soon enough, it was time for Mr Abrams and his sons to head to synagogue. Once all the men were ready, they left the house.

The synagogue was occupied by dozens of its members. Whilst outside was darkening, the synagogue was filled with light, joyous singing, and radiant, smiling faces. At some point during the middle of the service, Isaac's heart ignited with the joy of the spirit of Shabbat, and he was even more comforted after the pain from the nostalgia.

But Isaac later realised that neither Eliezer, Simon, nor Ariel bothered to come to synagogue throughout the weekdays or on Shabbat, and it brought his heart down low to be there to welcome Shabbat amidst their absence, but he pushed those thoughts away for now, for it depressed his spirit and he wanted to rejoice in honour of Shabbat.

Isaac sat in the third row towards the front in the centre-left section of the sanctuary. He sat near the edge, with his father and Mordechai to his right. The evening service proved to be rather packed, and about fifteen minutes in, someone sat to his left, which was a rare thing. He was too focused on his prayers to see who it was. At some point towards the end of the service, he took a peek and saw that it was a stranger who looked to be around his age. He wanted to welcome him, but he had to focus on his prayers. He hoped that he would have the opportunity to do so, that the young man would still be there after the services were over.

After the service concluded, Isaac turned to his right to tell his father and brother Shabbat Shalom, and he turned to the left to do the same to the young man, but he had left his seat. He was now gazing at the interior design of the sanctuary, standing just a few metres away. Isaac wondered whether he was a newcomer or whether he had been attending the synagogue whilst he had been away. Judging by the way he admired all of the intricate details of the windows, the benches, and the wall of the women's balcony above, Isaac concluded that he was the former and, though he was not one to initiate conversation with strangers so easily, he prepared himself to be welcoming towards the stranger when Rabbi Levi Gold appeared.

'Shabbat Shalom, Isaac,' said Rabbi Gold, extending his right hand.

'Shabbat Shalom,' said Isaac, smiling as he shook Rabbi Gold's hand.

'Good to see you again, Isaac. How have you been? Simon tells me you had a really good time in Israel.'

'Yeah, I most certainly did,' said Isaac, checking to see if the young man had yet gone, and he was now walking down by the platform at the front of the synagogue. 'I'm actually going to be staying now; I'm done with the programme.'

'It's good to have you back,' said Rabbi Gold.

Isaac couldn't help but smile in Rabbi Gold's presence. For as long as he could remember, Rabbi Gold had always exuded kindness and gentleness. He had even encouraged Isaac to go to yeshiva in Israel.

'Thank you,' replied Isaac.

'I'm sure Simon would have loved to spend time with you. Right now, he's out at some other synagogue.'

'Is he?'

'Yes. He's been going around checking out different synagogues on Shabbat. I think he wants to see what's out there if there's something else for him, you know?'

'Right.'

'Yeah. Well, all right. I'm sure I shall see you around again soon.'

Rabbi Gold left.

Now Isaac was wondering where Simon could be and whether Eliezer and Ariel could be with him.

For a second, he thought he had lost sight of the young man, dressed in a white dress shirt and khaki trousers (such was not an uncommon sight in this synagogue on a weekday, but not on Shabbat), but then saw that he had just sat down on an adjacent bench.

Isaac finally approached him.

'Hello, Shabbat Shalom,' said Isaac, extending his hand towards him. 'What's your name?'

"Ello, my name is Loïc,' he said, shaking Isaac's hand.

Isaac had never heard of such a name before, but his accent suggested that he was French.

'I'm Isaac Abrams. Where are you from?'

'I'm from Paris.'

'Are you new here?'

Loïc got up from the bench to stand whilst speaking to him. 'No, I am just visiting.'

'Have you got a place to eat?'

Loïc looked bewildered.

Seeing that Loïc was taking too long to mention where he was spending the Shabbat evening meal, Isaac said, 'Would you like to come eat with us? I could ask my parents whether you could join.'

Loïc still looked a bit insecure.

'We would love to,' Isaac insisted.

Loïc smiled. 'Sure, thank you so much.'

'Great! I shall ask my father. I'm sure he'd say yes. I've just got to go and wish my rabbi a Shabbat Shalom.'

'Oh, yes, of course,' said Loïc, putting his hands in his pockets.

Isaac queued to speak to Rabbi Aharon Levy, and Loïc followed him. By now, most of the congregation had left the synagogue.

Four persons later, Isaac was next, and he and Rabbi Levy embraced.

'So good to have you back,' said Rabbi Levy.

'So good to be back,' said Isaac.

'I'm sure we shall hear all about your adventures in Israel,' said Rabbi Levy.

'Oh, absolutely,' said Isaac.

Rabbi Levy smiled. 'Good. I was just talking to your father. Your parents, Joseph and Rivka, are two very special people. I have such high regards for them.'

Isaac smiled.

Loïc's face went pale as he filled with trepidation after the mention of the exaltedness of his hosts. Isaac noticed this.

Rabbi Levy clasped Isaac's hand in his hands. 'Please do me the honour of sending my regards to Rivka.'

'I shall,' said Isaac, nodding.

Mordechai was speaking to some of his friends, and then he went home. The Abrams lived five minutes away by foot. Mr Abrams continued to speak to some of the adults towards the back of the sanctuary, close to the way out. He would've gone, but he saw the new face accompanying Isaac and – though it had never happened before – it meant the possibility of a new guest, and if not, at least the opportunity of welcoming someone to the neighbourhood.

Rabbi Levy turned to Loïc. 'What's your name?'

'Loïc.'

'And what's your surname?'

'Schwartz.'

'And where are you from?'

'I'm from Paris.'

'Oh, welcome,' said Rabbi Levy.

'He shall be eating by us tonight,' said Isaac.

'Fantastic,' said Rabbi Levy before turning to Loïc. 'You're in for a real treat.'

ISAAC ABRAMS

By now, there were only several people in the sanctuary. Mr Abrams concluded his conversation with a fellow congregant as Isaac and Loïc walked up the right aisle.

Mr Abrams greeted Loïc and they shook hands.

'Shabbat Shalom,' said Loïc, sounding as though he were tired of saying that phrase.

'Dad, this is Loïc. He's visiting from France. Would it be possible for him to join us in our Shabbat meal tonight?'

'Of course; you're most welcome,' Mr Abrams told Loïc.

As they left the synagogue, Mr Abrams joined in conversation with a congregant who had been schmoozing with a group of people outside, and the congregant joined the three of them on their way home.

Isaac was so excited that Loïc would be joining them for the Shabbat meal, though he still was unsure how to have a conversation with this visitor, so he walked beside Mr Abrams and his acquaintance and listened to their conversation, and Loïc, who looked both uncertain and nervous, indeed as if he were in a foreign country, did the same.

Mr Abrams's acquaintance wished them a good night and a Shabbat Shalom when they had reached home.

They walked up the front steps and were welcomed in by Mrs Abrams, who carried a wide smile.

The Shabbat candles were burning on a separate table next to the dining table, stationed against the wall that separated the living room from the kitchen. The dining table was set. As Isaac introduced Loïc to his siblings, Mrs Abrams, who had met him by the front door, discreetly stationed another chair on the side of the table farthest from the kitchen.

'Wow, you 'ave such a nice place,' remarked Loïc. 'It is so clean.'

'Thank you,' said Mr Abrams, knowing fully well that every member of the household had dedicated at least a full hour to cleaning it earlier that day.

'Thank you so much for 'aving me,' said Loïc as Mrs Abrams returned, standing next to her husband.

'You are very welcome,' said Mrs Abrams.

'You're going to need this,' said Mr Abrams, placing a kippah on Loïc's head.

Loïc still had a lost look on his face. Isaac considered assuring him they weren't kidnapping him but thought it best not to.

Without any further conversation, they took their seats around the table to make kiddush. Loïc sat between Mordechai to his left and Isaac to his right, facing the girls, and Mr Abrams sat next to Isaac at the head of the table, and Mrs Abrams next to Mordechai, her end closest to the windows and opposite her husband. They washed hands (Isaac was starting to wonder about Loïc's upbringing after having to teach him how to wash hands and say the blessing for washing hands and then drying them) and returned to the table to sit, where Mr Abrams said the blessing over the bread, to which they all answered 'Amen'.

Along with the bread and several choices for dips, Mrs Abrams summoned a tray of fried gefilte fish, which she gave to Sarah, who gave to Ruth sitting to her right, and then to Mr Abrams. The whole room now smelled of fried fish. Mr Abrams took some and passed it to Isaac, who took some and passed it to Loïc.

'What is this?' asked Loïc, taking the tray hesitantly.

'It's fried gefilte fish,' said Isaac.

'What is that?'

Did Isaac need to explain that it was fish mixed with matzah meal fried in oil? He thought not.

'Try it,' he suggested.

'OK,' said Loïc, taking one of the pieces and humming in contentment. 'This is really good. What is it made of?'

'Stuff,' said Isaac. 'Want some more?'

Loïc took another piece and then passed the tray to Mordechai.

'I'm guessing they don't have this stuff in France, do they?' asked Isaac.

'No, I don't think so.'

'Oh. Just gefilte?' asked Isaac.

Loïc looked down at his plate, managing the slice of challah bread, hummus, sliced gherkin, and coleslaw he had taken. 'I don't know what this is.'

'You don't know what gefilte is?' asked Mrs Abrams.

'No, what is that?'

'Every Jew knows what gefilte is,' said Mrs Abrams, giggling.

'I don't really know much about Jewish food. I did not grow up religious,' admitted Loïc.

Isaac was suddenly filled with excitement. 'Is this your first Shabbat meal?'

'Yes.'

Mrs Abrams asked the girls to help her take out the dishes of the main course.

Having finished their chicken soup, they brought out potato pudding, Israeli salad, sweet-and-sour meatballs, and savoury noodle pudding. The place smelled of cooked potatoes.

Isaac saw how Loïc eyed the food set before him.

'Not a bad place to start, is it?' teased Isaac.

'No,' said Loïc.

Throughout the course of the meal, Loïc's head turned left and right, answering the questions the Abrams family darted at him from all directions. Eventually, Isaac monopolised the Ministry of Curiosity, and his other family members gave way to let him do so. It was not often they had a guest at the Shabbat table, much less so for him to be foreign-born and for him to have been brought up secular on top of that. Loïc Schwartz had become the fascination of this household.

Isaac was fascinated that Loïc had spent his first Shabbat meal at his place and that all this started with his initiation to make him feel welcome at the synagogue.

After reciting the grace after meals, Loïc said, 'Thank you all so much for the meal. I am so grateful, thank you.'

'You're so welcome,' said Mrs Abrams.

'Our pleasure,' said Mr Abrams, nodding. 'You're welcome to join us tomorrow.'

'Thank you,' said Loïc.

Mr and Mrs Abrams put the dirty plates and glasses away. Mordechai went to his bedroom as Sarah and Ruth carried their conversation into Sarah's bedroom upstairs.

Isaac kept Loïc with a few more questions and was pleased to hear his suggestion that they continue their conversation on the sofa by the windows, which displayed pavements mostly free of pedestrians and streets only occupied by some non-Jews who lived nearby and were still driving on Shabbat.

'Really, really nice place,' said Loïc, looking around.

'Thank you,' said Isaac. 'Your family isn't religious?'

'No.'

'And were they always in Paris, your ancestors?'

'My grandparents were from the Alsace region in France. They were actually more traditional. Then, my parents moved to Paris, where I was born, and they aren't religious, so I wasn't raised with the religion.'

Isaac was pleased to see that Loïc was more open with him in his responses here than at the table with everyone else. Loïc raised his shoulders at times as he spoke.

'So, you weren't circumcised?'

'No.'

Isaac couldn't imagine it; no bar mitzvah, no Torah learning, no Jewish school; how could a Jew live like this? He started to feel much compassion for him.

'How does it feel to be raised irreligious?' asked Isaac.

Loïc shrugged. 'Fine, I guess. Where are your family origins?'

'My great-grandparents came from Poland with their parents,' said Isaac. He took this question to possibly imply that he was tired of elaborating on all of the things he hadn't done in life, so he asked him, 'So what brought you to the synagogue?'

'I don't know. I was just walking around. My brother wanted to stay in the 'otel. We walked a lot today, so he was tired. It was getting dark, and I had never been in a synagogue, but I saw the synagogue and it looked very beautiful, so I decided to come and check inside.'

'That was the first time you had ever been in a synagogue?' said Isaac in amazement.

'Right. We weren't raised religious.'

'Wow, so your Jewish soul was yearning to go to the synagogue,' observed Isaac in awe.

'No,' corrected Loïc, 'it just looked very pretty, so I just went to check it out. I mean, I'm Jewish, but that is not why I went.'

Isaac felt so honoured to witness so many firsts for Loïc, both his first time at a synagogue and his first Shabbat meal.

'Who else are you travelling with?'

'Just my brother.'

'And what is he doing?'

'I don't know. I can check,' said Loïc, leaning to the side to reach for something in his pocket.

Isaac, alarmed that he was possibly reaching for his mobile phone, extended his hands forward and insisted, 'No, no, it's OK!'

Loïc, frozen and suspecting he had committed a faux pas, sat back up.

'So, what would you have done tonight, had you not come to us for Shabbat?'

Loïc shrugged again. Isaac hoped he wasn't annoying him with his questions. Indeed, every member of his family had bombarded him with questions.

'I don't know; I probably would 'ave gone to eat at some restaurant or something.'

'A non-kosher restaurant?'

'Yeah,' said Loïc, looking down and getting up from the sofa.

'I'm sorry if I've been too nosy; I'm just genuinely curious,' said Isaac as he also got up.

'No, I should go. I am getting quite tired anyway.'

Isaac escorted, or rather followed, Loïc to the entrance and then to the front door.

'I shall see you tomorrow then, right?' asked Isaac.

'I don't know. I shall probably do some things with my brother. We are going back to France on Sunday. It's our last full day, so thank you so much, really, for everything. It's been such a pleasure.'

'You're so very welcome,' said Isaac, shaking his hand as he held open the front door.

'Bye,' said Loïc as he descended the front steps.

'Shabbat Shalom,' said Isaac.

He watched for a bit as Loïc walked down the pavement, and then he closed the door. Immediately upon re-entering the living room, he wondered why he hadn't reiterated that Loïc was welcome the next day for lunch. Why hadn't he told him what time lunch was the next day? But then, he remembered that his father had told him that he was welcome.

What a respectful young man, thought Isaac. He would love to see him again the next day.

Then he thought, if he hadn't come over, he would have gone out to eat non-kosher food somewhere. Not only that, but he was also the reason Loïc was able to fulfil the commandments of hearing kiddush and eating a meal on Shabbat – and his first one! He had helped his fellow Jew stay away from such sins and observe such commandments. This was all because he had the idea to invite him for Shabbat and acted upon it! He had never felt so proud.

And then he remembered that Loïc had forgotten to return the kippah, but he knew that there were plenty more in the house and that Mr and Mrs Abrams wouldn't have minded if he had kept it as a souvenir.

CHAPTER VI

The Abrams family must have scared off poor Loïc, Isaac was sure, for he didn't show up for the next day's meal. Loïc had mentioned he wanted to go out with his brother, but Isaac had a feeling that the reason why he didn't show up was partly due to his family (himself included) making him feel uncomfortable with their insatiable curiosity. Before Loïc had arrived for dinner, he had already seemed a bit anxious, but still somewhat excited. Afterwards, he appeared fatigued, insecure, and uninterested. Still, Isaac was sad not to spend Shabbat with him.

Throughout the next week, Isaac looked forward to a quiet Shabbat dinner with his family after synagogue services. However, Sarah and Ruth made plans to spend Shabbat at their friends' places, and this was not without its consequences.

While Isaac was reading through the weekly Torah portion in his bedroom Friday afternoon, his mother called for him from the kitchen. He thought it was rather odd, as she didn't normally yell but would enter whichever room he was in and speak softly with him. He appeared there to find her with all the pots and pans and other kitchenware she had taken out, and she was sweating and red. She seemed a bit out of breath. He only saw her like this when preparing for a Shabbat or festival meal; otherwise, she was always tranquil.

'Isaac, I need you to do me a favour and go to the supermarket and fetch me these things. Sarah and Ruth aren't around to do it for me, and you're the only person home who can. I need these as soon as possible.'

She handed Isaac what initially appeared to be a hieroglyphic note, but upon further inspection and after what she had said, he presumed it to be a shopping list. He squinted, trying to determine whether it was in English or Hebrew, and then remembered that his mother was not fluent in Hebrew. He looked at her perplexedly.

Mrs Abrams turned away from the chicken soup she was attending and saw her son was still there, staring at her.

'OK. Shabbat starts in less than four hours, and I need these ingredients. Off you go!'

Isaac swallowed, wondering if they would have a proper meal this Shabbat.

As he made his way to the supermarket, pulling the shopping trolley, he had a sudden compassion that he had never felt before for his sisters and for Mordechai, who did the shopping before they were able to. He wondered what the intended plan of all his Shabbat meals since childhood had been compared to the resulting product. For all he knew, maybe his mother's dishes had never turned out the way she had wanted because his sisters had kept buying the wrong ingredients due to her messy handwriting. Such were the effects of walking the distance from his home to the supermarket with the shopping trolley alone, these meditations being unlike the conversations his sisters would've enjoyed having together on more profound subjects such as make-up and dresses until he finally reached Gan Eaten, which was where everyone hoped to get to at some point.

He commenced the dismal assignment by pulling out the dreadful shopping list. He was successful with the first three entries (eggs, flour, salt), going from one end of the supermarket to the other as the items were organised by the order of his mother's recollection and not by aisle. Though he was able to make out the fourth entry (five onions), he could not find them. Remembering he only had so much time, he left the shopping trolley by the wall and searched through the aisles for an employee whom he could ask for help. Shoppers buzzed around everywhere, all hoping to purchase their ingredients in time for the upcoming Shabbat and all the guests they would have at their meals.

Past the end of an aisle, where the next section was, he encountered a young man who looked to be about a year younger and was carrying a box of potatoes. The man was stockier than Isaac, a bit shorter, and with short, brown hair.

'Excuse me,' said Isaac, 'sorry, can you tell me where the onions are?'

'Sure, I'm going there right now,' he said, sounding as though he were struggling a bit with the weight of the potatoes, though he still carried an amiable countenance.

Isaac followed him to where he laid the box of potatoes on the ground. Nearby, he pointed out to him where the onions were, which was right by the red peppers, not too far from where Isaac had been.

'Thank you so much.'

'You're welcome,' he said, smiling.

Isaac hesitated and then asked, 'Do you mind if I just ask you another question?'

'Not at all,' he insisted.

Isaac pointed to one of the scribbles on the list. The young man drew closer to take a look.

'Could you tell me what this says?'

'Garlic,' he said.

'Oh, cheers, mate. I would've come home with grapes. What about this?'

'Pepper,' he said, then laughing. 'You can't read your own handwriting?'

As the young man went red laughing, Isaac, laughing anxiously, held his tongue in honour of his mother.

'Thank you, that's pretty much it. You've been very helpful,' said Isaac, looking at his name tag. 'Benjamin.'

Benjamin nodded.

'You're very welcome. You can just call me Ben. What's your name?'

'Isaac Abrams.'

'That's a nice Jewish surname,' said Benjamin.

'What's your surname?' asked Isaac.

'Jacobs,' replied Benjamin.

Isaac was sure with such a surname and appearance that Benjamin was Jewish, but the man wasn't wearing a kippah and he wanted to make sure. 'Are you Jewish?'

'Yeah. I recently started working here. I needed a job, and figured, why not work at a Jewish supermarket? And they took me in. I guess those are the benefits of being Jewish,' he said, grinning.

'Were you raised religious?'

'Oh, not at all. I've always been really curious about the religion, though.'

'Oh,' uttered Isaac, nodding his head. He then remembered that he was pressed for time. 'Well, I've really got to go. Thanks so much again for your help.'

'You're welcome.'

'Shabbat Shalom,' said Isaac.

'Shabbat Shalom,' said Benjamin, turning to pick up the box of potatoes to pour it over the pile of other potatoes for sale.

Isaac rushed through the supermarket as he continued searching for the remaining items on the list. He would have spoken more with Benjamin, but he couldn't. He did think, in the short amount of time he was able to, that it was interesting to have met a young Jew who wasn't raised religious but was interested in learning more about the religion.

Mrs Abrams was, with Isaac's help and God's abundant mercy and compassion, able to finish her meals as planned.

CHAPTER VII

As far as Isaac knew, this coming Shabbat was going to be the one spent with just the family, as he had hoped Shabbat would be ever since he returned home now that Sarah and Ruth were here. His sisters did the shopping for Mrs Abrams, and he was able to finish the weekly Torah portion in his bedroom before Shabbat came.

After synagogue services, long after it had become dark outside, Isaac walked home with Mr Abrams and Mordechai. Just as he approached the front of his house, he heard a familiar voice call out to him.

Isaac turned to his left and saw that it was Thomas, who was sitting on the front steps of his house. He descended the steps and greeted them. Mr Abrams and Mordechai stopped to greet him.

'What brings you out here?' asked Isaac.

'Just wanted some fresh air, to look around, and think. Nothing like the nice, hot summer air at night.'

'Oh, right,' said Isaac.

Mr Abrams and Mordechai continued going home, letting Isaac speak with his friend privately.

'I've just come back from York,' said Thomas.

'Oh, how was it?' asked Isaac.

'Great. It was so good to see my sister again. Anyway, where are you guys coming from?'

'Synagogue.'

'Oh,' uttered Thomas, his jaw hanging. He stared at Isaac attentively as if more information had to come.

'It's Shabbat, or the Jewish Sabbath, so we've just come back from services.'

'Right, but don't you guys have the Sabbath on Saturdays?'

'Well, no. We have it from Friday at sunset to Saturday at nightfall.'

Thomas's eyes widened. 'Wow, amazing. So, what happens now? What do you guys do?'

Isaac had to think about it, as this was something he had always taken for granted. 'Well, we have three meals, we go to synagogue, we sit together and talk, study Torah –'

'What's Torah?' asked Thomas.

'It's basically all of Judaism,' said Isaac. 'There are so many subjects to learn. Philosophy, the Bible, character development, or mussar, as we call it.'

'That's just so amazing. Are you going to study Torah now?'

'Well, actually, we're going to have dinner. It's the first Shabbat meal.'

'Wow, that's so interesting,' said Thomas. 'I would love to come and join you – if that's allowed?'

'Sure, you don't have to be Jewish to come,' said Isaac. He felt bad leaving Thomas there. He could see that Thomas seemed eager to join them. He added, 'I could ask my parents if you could come over.'

'Oh, would you? Yes, please. That would be amazing!'

'OK,' resigned Isaac. 'I shall go ask. You can follow me up to the top of the steps if you'd like.'

Isaac wasn't sure about the whole thing. He considered Thomas a highly refined young man and had been looking forward to spending time together, but he just couldn't see why a non-Jew would be so interested in partaking in the Shabbat meal; there was no obligation. Nevertheless, he answered his many questions along the way.

'So, what exactly does the Sabbath represent? What's the meaning behind it?'

'The Sabbath commemorates the seventh day of creation,' answered Isaac. 'On it, we remember that God created the world and how he rested on the seventh day after the six days of creation. So, in a way, we're attesting to that fact.'

'Whoa.'

Isaac ascended the steps. He would've elaborated further, but he entered the house alone and had to ask his parents whether Thomas could join them.

Everyone else was already standing around by the table. The candles were still burning, and the living room was luminous. He went up to Mrs Abrams.

'Mum, do you mind if Tom from next door joins us for dinner? He said he'd like to come.'

'Not at all,' she said.

'Tom wants to join us?' asked Mr Abrams, surprised.

'Yeah,' said Isaac, shrugging.

Isaac returned to Thomas, who had been waiting at the top of the steps, and held the door open for him, saying, 'You're most welcome.'

'Wow, thanks,' said Thomas, grinning as though he were travelling whilst on holiday again, even though it was a regular Friday night for him and he was just next door.

Mrs Abrams had already placed a chair between Isaac and Mordechai's places, similar to when Loïc had been there.

'Thanks so much for having me,' said Thomas.

'Our pleasure to have you,' said Mrs Abrams. 'We were surprised to hear you were interested in joining us.'

'Yes, this whole Shabbat thing is very interesting,' said Thomas.

So, they all stood by their seats as Mr Abrams flipped the pages through his prayer booklet to find the text for the kiddush blessing over the silver-coloured ritual cup of wine he held in his hand.

Thomas, who stood to Isaac's left, turned to him and asked, 'What's happening now?'

'Dad's about to recite the blessing over the wine. We do this every Shabbat.'

'Oh. OK.'

They all heard the blessing and responded with 'Amen' to Mr Abram's conclusion. Even Thomas responded with 'Amen', though he didn't have to. Isaac considered letting him know that he wasn't obligated to do everything they were doing, as he acted as though he were, but he at least admired that he was being respectful. He even followed them to the kitchen to wash their hands. Isaac wondered whether he would require a prayer booklet for reciting the grace after meals and whether he would recite the whole text should he insist on participating.

'What happens now?' asked Thomas as they all queued for the sink.

'Right now, we wash hands and wait for Dad to recite the blessing for the bread at the table, to which we respond, "Amen".'

Thomas nodded.

Isaac couldn't help himself. He just didn't want Thomas to feel as though he had to do all of this if he didn't want to.

'By the way, you don't have to wash and everything. You could just eat when we start eating.'

'No, it's OK; I don't mind,' said Thomas, then wondering, 'May I if I wanted to?'

'Sure,' said Isaac, 'I'm just saying you don't have to.'

So Thomas washed his hands and repeated the blessing for washing hands after Isaac, who taught him how to say it. Isaac stared oddly ahead as he followed Thomas back to the dining table, the latter of whom hummed merrily as he made his way back.

Once they had all sat down, Mr Abrams recited the blessing for the bread, and they all ate a slice of challah.

Thomas ate his slice and hummed in delight. 'Did you make this, Mrs Abrams?'

Mrs Abrams smiled and nodded. 'With the help of my daughters.'

'What made you want to join us for the Shabbat meal?' asked Mr Abrams.

'I don't know. I just find religion fascinating. I was just curious to know what it looked like and how Jews would celebrate Shabbat. It's very peaceful.'

Mr Abrams smiled. 'I'm glad you think so.'

Thomas continued, 'I was imagining perhaps music and dancing. I wasn't quite sure what this religious festival would entail, but I do enjoy the peaceful environment.'

'Right, well, we wouldn't be able to play music, apart from singing,' said Mr Abrams.

'Why?' asked Thomas.

'We can't play musical instruments on Shabbat because should they get damaged, we wouldn't be allowed to repair them, and electronic instruments can't be used because we're not meant to operate electronic equipment,' said Mr Abrams.

'Fascinating,' said Thomas.

Isaac observed Thomas's calm countenance and saw that he not only looked satisfied with his question being answered but by the information granted in the answer itself.

They moved on to the next course, the chicken soup, and they would stay on this one for a while.

It was like God was granting them atonement this Shabbat for the other Shabbat when Loïc had been their guest. Rather than flood their guest with questions, Thomas bombarded them with questions. It started when Mr Abrams, with good intentions, decided to share some thoughts he had learnt earlier on the weekly Torah portion. Thomas would not let one unfamiliar concept go by without seeking information on it. Isaac was starting to wonder whether he had been working on a new British encyclopaedia during his downtime. For the next twenty minutes or so, Mr Abrams, due to his own planned discourse and Thomas's enquiries, covered the weekly Torah portion, Rashi's commentary on it, who Rashi was himself, the five books of Moses itself, as well as Moses, the events at Mount Sinai, and dreidels.

As the rest of the family starved, Mrs Abrams and her children brought the dishes to the table. Just when Isaac had thought the atonement was over, Thomas asked Mr and Mrs Abrams about every dish on the table, its historical background, and its possible religious significance, and shared his knowledge of sweet-flavoured meat being consumed in traditional Jewish cuisine (Mrs Abrams had made sweet-and-sour meatballs).

Isaac was starting to get a little annoyed at all the questions. Were they all necessary? Because Thomas would enquire about every unfamiliar concept, and every response that Mr and Mrs Abrams would supply contained one, two, or three unfamiliar concepts, logic necessitated that the cycle would never end. He wished that they would not give such elaborate answers. He had yet to hear a yes-no question.

He had also wished that Loïc had shown a tenth of such enthusiasm. Loïc was Jewish! And yet, here was this non-Jew who sought to learn about everything Jewish. It was like the non-Jewish world suddenly wanted to learn more about Judaism than secular Jews did, and that thought made him sad.

He also wanted to talk to his sisters about Benjamin and what kind young man the new employee at the kosher supermarket they frequented was, but he didn't want to change the conversation so abruptly. He hadn't had the opportunity to bring it up earlier in the week.

'Were you brought up religious?' asked Mrs Abrams.

Isaac saw the neutral expressions on his sisters' faces. The whole Shabbat conversation by the table mostly involved either Mr and Mrs Abrams or Thomas. It was like Isaac and his siblings had accidentally stumbled their way into a foreign place that was their own home.

'My parents grew up Anglican. I think I may have been baptised, but I was not raised religious,' said Thomas, 'but I do find religions rather fascinating.'

Mrs Abrams then started talking about how she thought that it was interesting that there were so many religions. Isaac seized an opportunity during a long pause to ask his sisters, 'Have you guys met the new guy working at Gan Eaten, Ben?'

Sarah thought for a moment, shaking her head, and Ruth looked a bit lost.

'He's a bit short, with brown hair, young,' added Isaac.

Ruth nodded. 'Oh, yeah, I started seeing him there a few weeks ago. He's new.'

'Oh, I haven't noticed him,' said Sarah.

'He's a nice guy,' said Isaac.

'I've seen him, but I haven't met him,' said Ruth.

'It was so interesting. He said he grew up secular but wanted to learn about Judaism.'

'OK,' said Mrs Abrams excitedly.

Seeing that there was not much more to be said on this subject, Mr and Mrs Abrams decided to conclude the already-extended Shabbat meal. They recited the grace after meals. Thomas indeed asked for a prayer booklet and recited not only the blessings for the meal with bread, but also the blessings for Shabbat, as indeed he knew it was Shabbat, as well as for Hanukkah, Purim, Rosh Chodesh, Sukkot, Shavuot, Rosh Hashanah, and Passover, etc. Indeed, Thomas was having a festive time. Isaac hadn't noticed this while he was reciting. After the family had cleared the table, and Isaac was held back by the delay caused by his neighbour's recitation of the blessings, he stopped him and explained that he didn't have to recite the blessings for the other foods.

Mordechai was the only other person in the living room, and he was reading on the sofa.

Isaac sighed as they stood by the door which led to the entrance.

'Well, I hope you had fun,' said Isaac, stretching his arms.

'I most certainly did,' said Thomas. 'Thank you so much for having me. Please thank your parents on my behalf. I wasn't able to thank them personally. I have a deep appreciation for the Jews. I studied history at Cambridge, and I covered quite a bit of Jewish history in my independent study. I am fascinated by the culture and religion. I hope I haven't come across as too overwhelming with all my questions.'

'No, not at all,' lied Isaac.

'Very well,' said Thomas, smiling, the lights of the living room reflecting in his green eyes. He shook hands with Isaac. 'Thanks again. I hope to see you again soon,' he said as they proceeded to the front door.

'You're welcome,' said Isaac as he held the door open. 'I hope to see you soon, too.'

'Have a good night,' said Thomas, bowing his head before descending the front steps.

'You too,' replied Isaac, refraining from responding with the habitual 'Shabbat Shalom'.

Isaac closed the front door, shrouded now in the darkness between the front door and the door to the living room. In this small space, he enjoyed the moment of solitude. And then, the idea hit him – he had been doing it wrong all along. He had observed Thomas's enthusiasm, his curiosity. With regards to his friends, he had been so keen on figuring out what catalyst had driven them away from Judaism, but what he had to do was rekindle their interest and get them to realise just how essential and meaningful their religion was – but he would have to do so privately, one-on-one; he remembered how uncomfortable they had been whilst sharing their experiences at Chaim's Pizza, and he felt that they would be too embarrassed and submissive to peer pressure to lean into their potential interest in Judaism if done in a group. For the moment, however, he was very fatigued.

He collapsed onto his bed and instantly fell asleep.

CHAPTER VIII

During the Jewish month of Elul, the bulk of which coincided with September, Isaac didn't see his friends once. Week after week passed by, and they were still too holy for synagogue.

Isaac spent most of his days studying at home, but he was starting to become anxious. He still did not know what he would study or work as. He did not want his mother or father to confront him about this again.

He wondered how he would approach his friends one-on-one. What was he to do? Where were they to go? Eliezer was probably too busy with work, Simon with his preparations for auditions, and Ariel was probably starting university any time now. He found solace in those long, blissful hours when he would study Torah in his bedroom, the window to his right letting in light from outside as the silky, white curtains drifted in the wind.

During the evening service for Rosh Hashanah, he caught sight of all three of them. He was so happy to see them. Eliezer and Ariel prayed in the last row closest to the way out on the left side of the sanctuary, the same side where Isaac was. Simon prayed a few rows ahead of Eliezer and Ariel, thus closer to Isaac. This was where they usually prayed when they used to attend services regularly. Isaac meant to speak to them and wish them a good and sweet year, but as their places of prayer were scattered throughout the back section of the sanctuary, he was only able to see them as they exited together after he finished praying. He hurried towards the way out of the synagogue, briefly exchanging greetings for the new year and blessings with some of his fellow congregants along the way, until he emerged from the synagogue, and they were nowhere in sight.

They attended the Rosh Hashanah morning service as well. Isaac tried to contain his excitement and focus on the prayers throughout the service, which lasted for several hours. Again he missed them.

Isaac accepted that he was probably not going to speak to his friends until after the High Holiday services, or at least until after Rosh Hashanah, and it was forbidden to call them using his mobile phone during Biblical festivals, but he enjoyed that they were showing up. It gave him hope and evidence that they hadn't completely detached themselves from religious observance.

The lack of contact did not last long. After the morning service for Yom Kippur, Simon appeared in the aisle to Isaac's left.

'How's your fast going?' asked Simon once Isaac had closed the prayer book.

Isaac was delighted to see Simon. 'Pretty well; I'm used to it.'

'Not me.'

They ambled up the aisle and spoke by the sanctuary doors.

'How have you been? It's been a while,' said Simon.

Isaac thought it was sad; it had been a while, despite having been in London for a month and a half now.

'Fine. I've been studying a lot. How about you?'

There were only a handful of congregants scattered throughout the sanctuary now. All they had to look forward to were many hours of fasting and repentance ahead.

'I've been auditioning a lot, still nothing, hanging out with friends on the weekends.'

'How's your synagogue experience going?'

Simon's eyes grew wide. He looked shocked.

'My what?'

'Your dad mentioned you've been checking out different synagogues around on Shabbat.'

Simon's jaw dropped. He shuffled towards the way out with his hands in his pockets. 'I'm not, actually.'

'What do you mean? What have you been doing?'

'I – please don't tell my father, but I haven't been going to synagogue. I – I've actually been hanging out with friends. I've just been telling him that so he doesn't get worried.'

Isaac didn't need a mirror to see how red his cheeks were; he was fuming. His friend inclined his head towards the synagogue doors. Isaac went outside, the fresh air granting him some relief from his anger. Simon followed him to the top of the front steps. Isaac couldn't tell how much his hunger was influencing his behaviour, though he hadn't lost his awareness that this conversation had started off awkwardly, and that it wouldn't help him in his quest to encourage him to become religious again, which he intended to bring up later.

'I want you to know that I am very angry with you,' said Isaac, continuing even though Simon looked like he was on the brink of tears. 'I have a lot of respect for your father. What you're doing is just wrong. It's dishonourable.'

'I know. It's just...' At this point, Simon became speechless. He stared at Isaac helplessly, expecting him to continue the conversation.

Isaac's anger wouldn't go away, and now wasn't the time to bring up religion, so he led the way by descending the steps in silence and walking down the street. Over their heads, a blanket of thin clouds lay in the sky, greying everything around them a bit.

Isaac noticed that Simon's sulk had disappeared after they walked further down the street. 'Do you miss anything about the old days, Simon? I'm talking about before I went to Israel.'

'Oh, what year are we talking?'

'2005.'

They passed by a chippy. The smell of fish and chips gripped them. Isaac's stomach rumbled. He stared ahead, swallowing, as Simon inhaled.

Simon must have forgotten Isaac's question due to the aroma's distraction. He didn't respond until, finally, he said, 'I miss everything. The plays, the hangouts, sports. We had a lot of fun.'

'Anything about Judaism that you miss?'

After crossing the street, they passed by an Indian restaurant, and the smell of chicken tikka masala reached them.

Isaac's stomach rumbled again, and he said, 'Let's go there,' pointing to the upcoming turning on the left.

This time, Simon must have had to forget his question. Once he figured the silence had lasted too long, Isaac said, 'Simon?'

Simon turned to face him to his left. 'What?'

'I asked you what you miss about Judaism.'

'Oh, right, sorry. Well,' and just as Isaac was increasing in his anticipation of his answer, he said, 'I don't really miss anything in particular.'

'Nothing?'

Simon had the intellectual generosity – Isaac could admit even whilst fasting – to reflect on his response, before saying, 'No, not really.'

After this response, Isaac didn't quite know what to do. He was still feeling moody about what Simon was doing to Rabbi Gold, and his hunger was ruining his judgement. He figured he would pause his campaign for now; it probably wasn't a good time for Simon, either, since he was presumably fasting as well. He would wait for another day when he would feel well again, perhaps with a different member of The Team.

CHAPTER IX

Isaac had intended to ask Simon whether he would have wanted to join him and his family for a Shabbat meal sometime during their walk on Yom Kippur, but he had been so hungry and vexed that he had forgotten to.

After Yom Kippur, Isaac and Mr Abrams, with occasional help from Mordechai, built a sukkah in the garden.

On the first day of Sukkot, there were far fewer congregants in the synagogue than on Yom Kippur. Isaac didn't expect his friends to be among them. When he finished praying, he put away the prayer book, grabbed his lulav and etrog and after turning around, saw Ariel holding his lulav and etrog where he prayed towards the back, smiling and waving at him. As Simon and Eliezer weren't there, he figured that it would be the most opportune time to help Ariel become observant again – unless he already was.

'Chag sameach,' said Isaac.

'Chag sameach,' said Ariel, turning, and they both left the synagogue, where outside was warm and sunny. 'How have you been?'

'Thank God, you?'

'Good. Started school and everything. It's going all right.'

They walked down the street, and Isaac indicated to Ariel that he would walk him home so they could talk more. It normally took about ten minutes to walk to Ariel's house from the synagogue.

After talking about some current events, there was a moment of silence, which Isaac utilised to speak to Ariel concerning his observance. He wanted to know how he was doing spiritually and what would motivate him to become religious again.

How had that conversation gone with Simon again? What had he asked that seemed not to work? Isaac recalled asking him about the past when he had been more observant, so he figured he would focus more on the present.

'What's your favourite thing about Judaism?' asked Isaac.

Ariel, straight-faced as he looked ahead, paused for a moment and said, 'I think it helps bring people together.'

Finally, some progress, thought Isaac. 'How so?'

And then came that dreadful shrug, followed by, 'I don't know. I guess with Shabbat, the festivals, kiddush, it helps form a strong sense of community.'

Isaac recognised the importance of community, but was this the point of God administering all the commandments to the Jews? He wasn't sure whether he agreed with Ariel's prioritisation.

'What have you been up to?' asked Ariel.

Isaac hadn't wanted to change the subject so quickly. 'Studying Torah.'

Ariel hummed. 'OK.'

Isaac gave Ariel a few seconds to continue this new topic of his studying Torah. They had passed Isaac's house and were beyond the halfway point to Ariel's house.

'Have you been studying?'

'For school, yes.'

'And what about Torah?'

Ariel sighed, blushing. He was still looking ahead. 'Not so much.'

Isaac felt that he was making Ariel feel unnecessarily uncomfortable, so he changed the subject by extending the offer to Ariel that he had wished to extend to Simon.

'Would you like to come over for Shabbat sometime?'

His face still unmoved, he said, 'Maybe. I shall think about it.'

Isaac wondered why there was such a lack of enthusiasm. He also wondered whether he would make eye contact with his friend ever again. He felt that he was making Ariel bored.

Then, he remembered how thrilled he was to have seen him come to synagogue this morning, seeing the lulav he was carrying in his hand.

'Do you know what the meaning behind Sukkot is?'

Ariel stopped, and Isaac was forced to do the same.

'Sorry, but I've got some school work, lots of catching up to do, so I've really got to go.'

'Oh, all right, then. I shall see you later,' said Isaac.

'OK, chag sameach.'

'Chag sameach.'

They had reached the corner on Ariel's street. Apparently, he really wanted to get rid of Isaac, cutting short the potential of their conversation, which could've lasted several metres longer.

Schoolwork on a festival? Was what he was doing even allowed? Would he be – God forbid – writing for an assignment or typing on a computer, activities that were all forbidden on the first day of Sukkot? The idea terrified him, but he also felt like this was probably an indication of the state of their friendship, that he would've ended the conversation so abruptly.

But then, he caught himself. He and Ariel had known each other for years – seven years to be exact – and he didn't need to worry so much about Ariel; he had mentioned that he had needed to work on things, so he had a reason to end the conversation so fast. Isaac then turned around and went home.

He didn't see Ariel the next day at synagogue or even later during the afternoon service. What had he done? Was he pushing his friends even further away from Judaism, God forbid? Was this like with Loïc when he didn't show up on Shabbat for lunch after having dinner at Isaac's house? Apparently, the Abrams family was very skilled at unintentionally making others less religious.

Now, all he had left was to try with Eliezer, and with how his campaign was going and his knowledge of his motivation and new way of life, he didn't have a particularly good feeling about this.

CHAPTER X

Thursday included the first day of Chol Hamoed Sukkot, when most types of work were permitted during Sukkot. The air was cool, and the sky was covered in light-grey clouds. The streets of Golders Green were relatively quiet as it was the middle of what, for most Londoners, would be a regular workday. Since today was not a holiday that carried the same restrictions as the first two days of Sukkot, and as there was not a commandment to eat two meals, the Abrams were mostly concerned with their affairs with work and education. Therefore, Isaac ate lunch in the booth in the garden alone after about three straight hours of studying. He ate a cheese sandwich with lettuce and had a glass of sparkling water. After reciting grace after meals, he rose from the chair and decided that rather than return to his studies, which he usually would do, seeing that this was his only daily activity, he would go for a walk.

He went through the house to descend the front steps on the other side. He turned right, thus commencing his walk, when Thomas, who was sitting on his front steps, shouted his name, waving.

Isaac greeted him back, and Thomas descended the steps, opening the black front gates to talk to him.

'How are you doing?' asked Thomas.

'Great, just thought I should get some fresh air. You?'

'I'm great,' said Thomas. 'What have you been up to lately?'

'Well, it's Sukkot, which is a Jewish festival. I'm just trying to get the most out of learning and stuff.'

'Wow. Is that why you've got that booth set up in your garden?'

'Yes,' said Isaac.

'Amazing,' said Thomas, putting his hands in his pockets. He moved a bit from side to side as he stood before Isaac as if trying to contain his excitement. 'I saw that you had it when I was looking out my window. You guys tend to set it up this time of year. I've always wondered why and meant to ask. I had assumed you just preferred eating outside.'

'Ah, no, we just have to eat food in the sukkah.'

'Why?' asked Thomas.

'It's just one of the commandments of this festival. It's from the Chumash. The Five Books of Moses.'

'Wow, amazing. And can a non-Jew eat in there?'

Isaac shrugged.

'Sure, I don't see why not.'

'Wow. Well, I don't want to interrupt you from your walk. I think I shall go back inside now. It was good to see you.'

'OK, you too,' said Isaac, and they waved goodbye to each other.

So Isaac headed down a rather busy street lined with various shops and other businesses on both sides. He turned left to go down a quiet street, intending to circle back home. It was down this street that he saw Eliezer walking ahead of him towards his direction.

Eliezer was looking down with his hands in his pockets. He had a bit of a hunch as he walked outside. He was much taller than Isaac. He had dark hair, a rather long face, and a rather long, pointy nose.

Eliezer caught sight of him as they were about to meet.

'Isaac!' said Eliezer, embracing him. 'How are you?'

'Good, just going for a walk,' said Isaac.

'Let me join you,' said Eliezer. 'Which way are we going?'

Isaac pointed ahead.

So, they walked together. Isaac felt he had always been the closest to Eliezer out of his other friends. He felt that Eliezer understood him the best, and he thought that Eliezer probably liked him the most out of the group, too. Whereas most of their hangouts included the four of them, Isaac had spent time one-on-one with Eliezer the most. Although they were quite different in both personality and abilities, Isaac had always secretly admired Eliezer's strength, determination, and honesty.

Now, after a few exchanges of polite pleasantries, it was time to bring up his religious observance. He had asked Simon about the past and what he missed, which was not productive. He had asked Ariel about the present and what he enjoyed about Judaism, which went nowhere. Now, he figured all he could do was ask about the future and maybe highlight the long-term consequences should Eliezer choose not to keep the faith. But what would he say? Then, he started to wonder, what if he had got the order wrong? These were three different people. They each had their unique desires and interests. What if bringing up the past would have worked on Ariel, the present with Eliezer, and the future with Simon? Nonetheless, he could not change the past, and he thought that his original idea of bringing up the future was the best one he had.

'What are your goals, Eliezer?'

'Hmm,' uttered Eliezer, 'to keep building my company, get more clients, make more money –'

'I meant in terms of spiritual goals.'

Eliezer paused, looking a bit confused, maybe a bit terrified even.

'Spiritual goals?'

Isaac hummed in affirmation, nodding.

'Well, I don't have any. Eat healthy, I guess, work on being healthy –'

'What about Jewish goals?'

'I haven't got any,' he said, looking at Isaac defeatedly.

They walked for another minute in silence.

'I haven't seen you in synagogue since Yom Kippur,' said Isaac, without looking at him.

Eliezer didn't respond.

Isaac was starting to feel a little bit upset and resentful. Which one he felt more, he couldn't tell. He withdrew the invitation for Shabbat he would have extended to him; he clearly wasn't interested in Judaism anymore. None of his friends were.

It didn't help that they had now reached the corner on Isaac's street, and Eliezer had to make a right to go to his place. Isaac wished for anything Eliezer could have said that would have been good.

'So, what have you been up to?' asked Eliezer, staring at Isaac with his dark eyes as they faced each other.

'Just studying Torah.'

'For yeshiva or for yourself?'

'Myself.'

'And what are your goals?'

Isaac was silent. This was the same question he had been asking himself, and he was humbled to respond, 'I don't know.'

They spoke for a while longer until a burst of rain proclaimed the end of their conversation.

CHAPTER XI

As the days passed, Isaac was starting to feel worthless and directionless. The clouds slumped heavy in the air, casting a grey pallor over the city. He thought about his time spent in Israel again. Though it had certainly rained there as well, it seemed as though his memories carried only sunny weather and endless opportunities for spiritual growth. He wondered, was he supposed to be in England? Was there someone he had to meet? Was he indeed meant to choose a job that would bore him, but facilitate his making a living to start his own family?

He no longer went out for walks to make himself feel better or come up with a plan; he'd feel the same way the next day and not come up with anything novel. His studying was starting to weaken. He'd learn for only a few hours a day and not have the same focus or will to keep reading as before. This was when he was starting to grow anxious. Studying Torah was less appealing? He knew something was wrong.

After the morning service that Sunday, he knew of only one person who would know the answer. Once he finished praying, he walked over to Rabbi Levy.

'Isaac, good morning, how are you?'

'I'm well, thanks, good morning,' said Isaac. 'May I speak to you about something if you have time?'

'Certainly,' said Rabbi Levy. 'What's up?'

Isaac felt better to see that there was no queue of people to speak to him.

'I'm starting to feel a bit stuck in life,' confessed Isaac. 'I just don't know what to do. My parents want me to study or find a job. I agree, I should, but I don't know what to do.'

'Every person has a unique purpose,' said Rabbi Levy, raising his index finger. 'Only you can determine what your purpose in life is. I can only help you find it.'

'Right. I'm not quite sure what that purpose is,' said Isaac, feeling bad as he was twenty-one years old.

'What are your interests? What are your passions? What are you good at? Answering these questions can help you find out.'

Isaac thought about it for a while.

Isaac didn't mention his interests included studying Torah. What was the point? He had to think of something his parents would approve of. He'd have to think of a well-paying career, and he was hoping that Rabbi Levy would help him determine that.

'I'm not sure if I'm particularly good at anything,' Isaac admitted. He was starting to grow suspicious that he was an exception to the rule that everyone had a unique purpose. If there had been something he had learnt at yeshiva, it was that Jewish law was full of many details and exemptions.

'I'm sure you are good at something,' said Rabbi Levy. 'You just have to try new things – what concerns you about the world? What problem bothers you that you would like to fix?'

Isaac could think of nothing other than his friends' decrease in religious observance. There was nothing other than his dilemma regarding his future career that bothered him, but he held his tongue. He was not going to speak ill of his friends, especially since Rabbi Levy knew them personally.

'Honestly, just that I know some Jews who are becoming less religious.'

'Then *that's* what you need to focus on,' said Rabbi Levy.

Isaac was lost. Was he saying that he would have to focus on making his friends religious again – and that his friends would pay him for it? He was so confused. He had been trying to do so, and it clearly wasn't working.

'Believe me, Isaac, unless you haven't been doing so already, pray to Hashem. Ask Him for guidance and ask that He put you in the right place so you can take the opportunity when He presents it to you – though I'm sure you have already.'

Isaac hadn't been doing so. He thanked him, and he figured that he had nothing to lose by taking his mentor's advice. He could never think of a scenario in which Rabbi Levy's words were unhelpful, as bizarrely confusing as the current situation was.

So, as he was still in the synagogue, he returned to his place of prayer and spoke to God. 'Hashem, please put me in the right place in order to achieve my true purpose in life. Please help me figure out what my true purpose in life is, and please stop my neighbour's dog from barking so loud; I can't study sometimes. Thank you for listening.'

With that, he walked home, clutching onto his bag holding his phylacteries as the wind carried cool air; autumn was really here.

During the walk, he meditated on what his purpose in life could possibly be, on what his rabbi had told him, on what the future could bring. Indeed, God could make anything happen. Yet, he still felt very hopeless. The silence of the neighbourhood helped him calm down.

He analysed the unspoken answers he had to Rabbi Levy's questions – he wanted to always learn Torah and he wanted to make his friends religious again. For the sake of progress, he put the money factor aside for a moment. Was there any connection between the two answers? What career could come out of this, one that he had the capability to pursue? He obviously couldn't keep studying in yeshiva, seeing that his parents wouldn't pay for another year (he wouldn't have asked them to, anyhow; he would've considered it taking too much advantage), so that was not possible, though he did solve that problem because he could study by himself. Now, what about the other question? He wanted his friends to become religious again. He had tried, and he failed, but there was a theme here, which was trying to make Jews who weren't religious become religious. His friends were no longer in the picture, but did he know of any other Jew who wasn't religious?

And that was when he thought of Benjamin Jacobs. Ben – from the supermarket! He had even told him that he was curious to learn about the religion! Yes, indeed, he thought – and the excitement of this purpose made him not care about the money – *this* was what he wanted to do! This was what he needed to do! God had put him in his life for this purpose; this was why they had met!

Isaac intended to go to the supermarket once Sukkot was over to offer his services to Benjamin of educating him on Judaism, free of charge.

CHAPTER XII

The same day, Isaac made a simple cheese sandwich for lunch in the sukkah. He washed his hands in the kitchen before going outside. Once he sat down before his lunch, his mobile phone rang. He saw that Thomas was calling. He said the blessing for the bread, took a small bite, drank a sip of water, and then answered just in time before the phone stopped ringing.

'Hello?' said Isaac.

'Isaac,' said Thomas excitedly. Isaac was expecting to hear good news.

'Hi,' said Isaac, 'how's it going?'

'Rather well, thanks,' said Thomas. 'It's Sunday, and we haven't really seen each other lately. I was wondering whether you'd like to hang out.'

'Sure,' said Isaac, 'though I am eating in the sukkah right now.'

'Can I join you?' pleaded Thomas.

'I haven't really prepared anything.' Isaac wasn't quite sure as to why Thomas would be so adamant about eating with him in the sukkah.

'It's OK. I shall bring my own lunch.'

'OK, though I'm not quite sure whether it would be kosher,' said Isaac. He would ask him not to bring non-kosher food, but only if Thomas misunderstood his subtle message.

'Then I shall come over without food. I don't mind. I could eat later.'

'Well, I could make you a cheese sandwich, but that's all I've got.'

'Sure, that's fine,' said Thomas.

'All right. So, I shall see you soon?'

'Yes, I shall be there in just a minute,' said Thomas.

So, Isaac got up and met Thomas on the front steps. He made him a sandwich in the kitchen, and they sat together in the sukkah, Thomas sitting to Isaac's left.

'Wow, this place is amazing,' said Thomas, admiring the wall and the leafy roof above. 'Don't I have to say a blessing on the sandwich?'

'Well, if you were Jewish, yes.'

'That's what I meant,' said Thomas. 'What would I say?'

'You'd normally wash hands first,' said Isaac.

'Could you remind me again how?' Thomas requested.

'Sure,' said Isaac, who led him back into the house, where in the kitchen he taught him how to wash his hands with the copper wash cup, what blessing to say, and what blessing to say over the bread back in the sukkah. A deep sense of satisfaction came upon Thomas's face after biting into the sandwich as if he were on a massage chair.

'Do you like the sandwich?' asked Isaac.

'I like everything,' said Thomas, nodding his head.

'So, what's new with you?'

'Just reading and stuff. I'm still thinking about what to do next.'

'Yeah, me too.'

Thomas looked down at his sandwich. Isaac really wanted to know why he was so keen on washing his hands and saying the blessings. Isaac was telling him about his being stuck in life. There was a brief moment of silence.

Thomas, after staring pensively at the surface of the wooden table, said, 'I want to tell you something. I've been thinking a lot about it lately, and I want to convert to Judaism.'

Isaac froze. He looked at Thomas's face, and he was looking at him with a serious expression. He barely gulped when Thomas continued. He immediately thought of his previous prayers. Was God answering his prayer so quickly? Was this his purpose in life, to teach Thomas about Judaism so that he could convert and become an observant Jew? But maybe this was wishful thinking. He didn't want to get his hopes up prematurely.

'I've been reading a lot about Judaism, and for a while now. I studied a lot about Jewish history at Cambridge. It made me think a lot about you and your family. I was reading a bit about the beliefs and became very curious about the religious aspect and how similar it is to Christianity. I couldn't stop reading, and when I went to your place for Shabbat, I fell in love with it. It was such a meaningful experience. I kept reading, just as an admirer, though wishing I could participate too, though knowing I couldn't become one.

'That was until I found out that one could convert to Judaism. I read brief summaries about the books of the Jewish Bible, and I found it fascinating that Ruth converted, but I thought that conversions were a thing of the past, that one could only do so during Biblical times, but after browsing through books about Judaism, I noticed there were parts dedicated to conversion – it *is* possible! So, I am determined to do so.'

Isaac stared at Thomas.

'You look shocked,' said Thomas. 'I don't mean to intimidate you. It's just… I know you and you're probably my only Jewish friend who's religious, so I wanted to tell you that. You and your family helped me realise that this is what I want.'

Isaac blushed. 'I'm glad to see we've left such a remarkable impression on you. I'm just a bit shocked because no one has ever told me this. I don't think I've ever met a convert before.'

Thomas smiled faintly after Isaac's statement, expecting to hear more after all the information he had shared.

'Well,' continued Isaac, 'I personally don't know how exactly one converts, but I can ask my parents. You have my full support, and I would even offer to teach you if this is something you really want –'

'It *is* something I really want,' Thomas assured him.

'Very well, then. I shall have to arrange a time with you. I do have plans to possibly teach someone else. Once that's settled with, I'd love to set up a time with you.'

'Thank you so much, Isaac. I really appreciate it,' said Thomas.

'You're very welcome,' said Isaac.

After the meal, they both recited grace after meals, and they chatted for a little longer before Thomas returned home.

When Isaac saw his parents later that day, he asked, 'Do you guys know anything about conversions? Tom next door wants to convert to Judaism.'

Mr Abrams looked up from the book he was reading on the living room sofa. Mrs Abrams passed through the opening to the kitchen, wiping her hands on the hand towel as her jaw hung.

'Thomas Bannister wants to convert to Judaism?' asked Mrs Abrams after several long seconds necessary for comprehension.

'Yes,' said Isaac.

Mr and Mrs Abrams exchanged looks of surprise.

'OK,' uttered Mrs Abrams as Isaac stood by the door leading to the back corridor. 'Well, to be honest, I've never met a convert before. I'm not quite familiar with the process.'

'I've met a couple of converts,' said Mr Abrams. 'I'm not sure of the whole process, but I do believe he would have to find a rabbi who would be sort of like a representative to guide him through the process and represent him in the Jewish court. I know Rabbi Levy helps supervise conversions, from what I understand.'

'Brilliant,' said Isaac. 'I was thinking of using the dining table as a place to teach some students who would be interested in learning about Judaism. Would that be all right with you?'

Mr and Mrs Abrams exchanged brief glances.

'Sure,' said Mr Abrams.

'Thanks.'

Isaac grinned as he turned around to walk back to his bedroom. He was so excited about teaching Thomas and Benjamin. He felt like his life was meaningful again. He had wanted to focus on teaching Judaism to Jews who were non-religious so that they could become religious, but he figured that teaching a prospective convert would be a similar task to undertake, and he thought it would be rather interesting.

He studied for a few hours, and later that day, it dawned on him as to how quickly God had answered his prayer from earlier that day.

CHAPTER XIII

After the evening service at synagogue, Isaac asked Rabbi Levy whether he would be willing to superintend Thomas's conversion. Rabbi Levy said he would be more than happy to but preferred to meet Thomas in person first.

Isaac shared this exciting news with Thomas, and he planned to meet him the next day. After the evening service that Monday, Isaac left the synagogue as Thomas spoke with Rabbi Levy. He couldn't wait to hear the news following their encounter.

Later that night, Thomas informed Isaac over the phone that Rabbi Levy thought that Isaac would be a suitable teacher for instructing him on the fundamentals of Judaism. Isaac said that he would like to arrange a time for lessons soon at his place. In his mind, Isaac intended to arrange a time to teach Benjamin first.

On Friday, Isaac set aside the Gemara he was studying. The white curtains of his bedroom window flowed in the air. He looked at his clock – it was five past noon. He got up from his desk and found his mother in the kitchen, where she was kneading dough for challah.

'Mum,' he said.

'Yes, dear?'

'Do you need any help with shopping? Shall I do the shopping for you?' he offered.

He would've gone to the supermarket to see Benjamin anyway, but he had figured he might as well ask.

Mrs Abrams gasped, turned around, and looked as though she were about to break down in tears.

'Oh, my boy, Isaac,' she said, her voice cracking, and she hugged him tightly, 'oh, how much yeshiva has changed you for the better! To honour your mother and father – that's the way one ought to live. In accordance with the Torah! You have no idea how touched I am!'

Isaac, whilst trapped in his mother's arms, refrained from mentioning that he never intended on bringing up this offer ever again.

She let go of him, tightened her apron, and said, 'All right. I would need a couple of minutes to come up with a list. – I haven't even started it! Come back in about ten minutes. Thank you so much, Isaac!'

'No problem,' mumbled Isaac as he left the kitchen.

Isaac was starting to wonder whether he should have even offered as he waited in his bedroom for those ten long minutes, which felt as if he were punished.

Ten minutes later, Isaac returned to the kitchen, where Mrs Abrams handed him the shopping list and he set off for Gan Eaten with the shopping trolley.

Upon entering the supermarket, he first rolled the shopping trolley around the perimeter of the supermarket and then up and down the various aisles. There was no trace of Benjamin. He figured he could ask the cashier whether she had seen Benjamin that day and, if so, where he could find him.

After forty minutes of shopping for fifteen items, he approached the cash register and placed the items on the conveyor belt.

'Excuse me,' he said to the cashier after placing the last item on the conveyor belt, 'Is Ben working today?'

'Who?'

'Ben. – Benjamin? I can't remember his surname.'

'Oh, no I haven't seen him. Actually, I think he's out today,' she said.

'Really?'

'I'm afraid so,' she said, nodding as she swiped the bananas over the scanner.

'When have you last seen him?'

'I can't remember. Not since Sukkot ended, that's for sure.'

'Do you know when he shall be coming back?' asked Isaac.

'I can't say I do, sorry,' she said, biting her lip.

'All right,' he said under his breath. He sulked. 'Thank you.'

He lifted the three bags of shopping and placed them into the shopping trolley. He then started rolling it.

'Are you going to pay for your shopping?' she asked.

'Oh, right, sorry,' said Isaac before handing her the fifty-pound note his mother had given him.

He tucked the change and receipt into his pocket, and they wished each other Shabbat Shalom.

Upon returning home, Isaac couldn't help but frown. He had missed his opportunity to learn with Benjamin. Why hadn't he exchanged contacts with him when they had first met? Why hadn't he offered to teach him before? He was confused. He thought that his purpose was to help non-religious Jews become religious again. His heart grew heavy. Had it not been for the imminent arrival of Shabbat, he would've surely felt very low. He felt as though he had missed a very important opportunity to teach Benjamin by not acting upon it when it had presented itself to him.

Now, he turned all his hopes and attention to Thomas. He was going to schedule a study session with him.

Their cholent that Shabbat did not feature beans or potatoes.

ISAAC ABRAMS

CHAPTER XIV

That Sunday morning, after attending the morning service at the synagogue and an hour of study, Isaac called Thomas to schedule a time to teach him this week. Seeing that they were both unemployed young men, they were available that day. They agreed to meet at three in the afternoon. Isaac spent some time going over what he would want to teach him. He gathered introductory sources that he had and some books from his father's library in order to draft a lesson plan. After seeing how this first session would go, Isaac intended to plan when and how often they would meet.

So, at three o'clock, Thomas rang the doorbell, and Isaac let him in. They greeted each other. Isaac was starting to feel a bit nervous. He was starting to wonder whether he was truly qualified to teach Thomas. Was he the appropriate gatekeeper to the knowledge of Judaism? Would he give Judaism a good first impression? And was he a good teacher after all? He led him to the dining table, which was where their learning session would take place. Thomas sat, listening to Isaac as he taught whilst standing. Isaac still couldn't believe that he was teaching a future convert, who was his neighbour and friend, Thomas, out of all people! He would have never guessed that Thomas from next door would one day want to convert to the Jewish religion.

Isaac started the session answering any questions Thomas had about Judaism.

Thomas asked about the reasons behind some of the laws of Shabbat, at what age men were supposed to get circumcised, and whether the conceptions of God by Muslims were congruent with Judaism. After talking over these questions and then going over briefly the denominations of Judaism, Isaac figured he had to stop in order to get through what he wanted to share; otherwise, by answering all of Thomas's questions, he would cover half of the topics he would bring up in all the sessions combined, and in a rather disorganised manner.

Isaac then started his planned part of the lecture, in which he would speak about the essence of God, how He was one, non-physical, and beyond space and time. He would have loved to move on to his next planned topic, which was the nation of Israel and its purpose, starting with Abraham and God's covenant with him, except that he would have to keep pausing from his discourse to answer Thomas's many questions, such as 'But why do Christians believe in the Trinity? Where did that come from?' and 'How did God speak to people if He's not physical?'

Isaac was starting to feel rather stressed. He hoped that he was hiding his shakiness well from Thomas as he stood before him. He thought for a brief second about sitting down, but standing helped him feel like he was portraying his intellectual dominance. He had planned his lesson out well, but Thomas's questions were making him feel thrown off course. It made him feel very uncomfortable, affecting his teaching and making him less coherent.

After going over a few topics, Isaac then came to the part of the session where he spoke about daily living. He had figured that combining Jewish thought with Jewish law would make an interesting combination. He went over saying 'Modeh ani', washing hands, and the blessing after relieving oneself in the toilet.

'So, this is the first thing you do every day?' asked Thomas, who had not come with a notebook or pen.

'Yes,' said Isaac, then laughing. 'You would be surprised, but there is even an order in which we do some things. We shall get to it, but, for example, one would put on the right side of a garment before the left. So, we'd put on the right shoe before the left, but when taking off our shoes, we'd take off the left shoe first.'

'So, we'd tie the right shoe before the left when putting on our shoes?' asked Thomas.

Isaac paused.

'Actually, no. We would tie the left shoe first before tying the right shoe.'

'But I thought that we were supposed to put on the right side of clothes first,' said Thomas.

Isaac was taken aback. He swallowed. He was trying to remember what he'd normally do in the morning, replaying it in his head. Indeed, he would tie his left shoe right after putting on the left shoe after putting on his right shoe. 'At least, that's what I do.'

'But why? Aren't you supposed to put the right side on first? Shouldn't you tie it first, too, before moving on to the left shoe?'

'I'm not sure,' Isaac admitted. He was now properly embarrassed. He stood there in silence. Then, he looked at his watch. It was half past four. He had intended the lesson to be an hour before continuing with his studies.

'Well, I think we shall end here for today. We've covered a lot of material.'

Thomas grinned as he got up from the seat.

'Great, I really enjoyed it. When's our next lesson?'

Isaac was relieved that Thomas was eager to have another session together. His face flushed; he was starting to feel like a fraud after being unable to answer his question. His embarrassment hadn't gone away.

'I shall let you know,' said Isaac, knowing he'd need some recovery before he could possibly plan material to cover in a second session with him, and after mustering up the confidence to create a new plan, to actually teach his student. 'I shall ring you at some point.'

'OK, great,' said Thomas.

Isaac escorted him to the front door. They bade each other goodbye, and once Isaac shut the door, he sighed, hunching with his back against the door.

Isaac's confidence in his teaching potential was draining. He couldn't believe he couldn't answer Thomas's question in the first session, and this had been supposed to be the most basic and fundamental; the future sessions, which would naturally be more complicated, would certainly bring scores of similar moments of humiliation. How did he expect to follow what he thought was his goal in life to help non-religious Jews like Benjamin become religious by teaching them if he clearly did not qualify due to his lack of knowledge?

After supper, Isaac was in the kitchen when Sarah asked, 'How did your lesson with Tom go today?'

'Oh, terrible,' said Isaac. 'He asked a question, and I had no clue what the answer was.'

In reality, Isaac had felt that it had been a quite blissful experience up until the question was asked; he hadn't realised how quickly time had passed.

'Oh, well, that happens, I guess,' she said, her arms crossed as she leaned back against the counter.

'No, you don't understand,' said Isaac. 'I'm not sure if I should keep teaching him. The lessons are going to get harder and harder. He also asks a lot of questions. Half of the questions he shall ask I'm going to answer with "I don't know." Don't you think he deserves a better teacher?'

'Isaac, no one knows everything. No teacher is ever expected to know everything. Isn't that part of the process, learning through your students? I'm sure every teacher started off just like you.'

Isaac nodded.

'I think you're right, Sarah. Thank you.'

'Of course,' she said, smiling.

So, later that night, Isaac called Thomas and scheduled their next lesson for Wednesday. He figured he'd give himself three days to do a little research and find out the answer to his question. He wasn't going to forget about it.

CHAPTER XV

By Monday, Isaac found the answer to Thomas's question, but he had already scheduled the second lesson to take place on Wednesday. He took advantage of the time he had before the next session. Rather than take only one hour in total for preparation, he took one hour on Sunday and Monday, two hours on Tuesday, and another hour on Wednesday. He couldn't believe he was doing this for free.

Thomas arrived for his next lesson on Wednesday at three. Isaac wanted to make sure that before he'd forget, he'd answer his question from before. So once Thomas was seated at the dining table and Isaac standing before Thomas to show his authority, he decided to answer.

'I wanted to mention, before we begin, that I didn't forget your question from before, and I wanted to answer it,' said Isaac.

'OK,' said Thomas, confused, having forgotten what that question was of the many that he had already asked.

'The reason why we tie our left shoe before our right shoe is because we wrap tefillin on our left arm – but we shall get to tefillin later.'

'Right,' said Thomas, nodding. He blinked, both indifferent and confused. He had forgotten about the order of putting on and taking off one's shoes, but it was good to know that he had to tie his left one first.

Isaac was starting to wonder whether Thomas even remembered asking such a question. Thomas looked a bit tired. Throughout the course of this session, Thomas barely asked a question. It was as if Isaac had to instil in him both enthusiasm and knowledge, the former of which could have aided the reception of the latter.

After an hour, Isaac saw that Thomas's countenance was a little inattentive today and his tone monotonous, so he ended the session, and Thomas thanked him for it.

Afterwards, Isaac thought, I'm being too hard on myself. Sarah was right; I don't have to know everything. He probably didn't even remember asking the question. Why am I so hard on myself? Just because I didn't know the answer to a question doesn't mean I can't teach.

So, Isaac's confidence received a boost, seeing that he truly wasn't expected to know everything. And today, though Thomas had asked a question or two, he was able to answer all of the questions, and the session went smoothly. It was thrilling to teach, though he did feel a bit bad that he had seemed a little less energetic today, but that hour flew by, and he had invited him to have another session the next day, which Thomas gladly accepted. Should that session go well, Isaac intended to have a lesson with him every day.

CHAPTER XVI

That next session went very well. Thomas was very excited. Isaac figured maybe he was just tired the previous day. He had a few more questions, and Isaac was able to answer all of them, and even if he didn't, that wouldn't have discouraged him so much anymore. Isaac then invited him to have a lesson every afternoon, Sunday through Thursday, and Thomas accepted. Isaac was very excited about this. He figured he'd still have Fridays to take a break from the lessons and do more planning, the latter of which he wouldn't want to do on Shabbat.

Isaac told Thomas about the afternoon and evening service for Friday. Ten minutes before the afternoon service started, Isaac, Mr Abrams, and Mordechai met Thomas outside their houses and walked to synagogue together where they would welcome Shabbat.

At the synagogue, Isaac, Mr Abrams, and Mordechai moved over a little bit to the right from their usual places so that Thomas could sit at the end of their row.

Thomas seemed to appear at ease whilst at synagogue. In fact, he seemed to be at home, smiling and looking around, admiring the details of the synagogue as if he were in a museum. Isaac didn't even have to guide him throughout the service; he would look at Isaac's prayer book to see what page they were on and recite the prayers, to Isaac's surprise. Isaac had intended to give him more details on the liturgy at some point later on during his learning.

Isaac looked around as the afternoon service started: still no sign of any of his friends. Every Shabbat he checked around just in case any of his friends would show up. He hadn't seen any of them since Sukkot, and it was now the beginning of Cheshvan, at the end of October. A part of him felt that they would turn up one of these days, but another part suggested that they wouldn't, and he should just accept this. Due to their long absence from his life, it almost felt as if they didn't live in the neighbourhood anymore. Or, as if they didn't exist.

After the evening service of Shabbat, Isaac decided to talk to Rabbi Levy about his friends. He wanted to know what he would suggest for his situation. How would he suggest he bring them back to Judaism? Surely, he was the right person to ask.

So, he queued to speak to him whilst Thomas conversed with Mr Abrams and Mordechai was around chatting with his friends.

Isaac didn't want to bad-mouth his friends, God forbid. He had to phrase his questions in a general way so he could mask his friends' identities and thus not reveal too much about their specific situations.

It was his turn to speak to Rabbi Levy.

They shook hands.

He thought before posing the question. 'I wanted to know your opinion about a certain situation. Let's say someone that someone was close to started becoming less religious. How would you deal with that? How would you encourage that person to come back to being religiously observant again?'

'Hmm, yes,' began Rabbi Levy, squinting whilst stroking his short black beard, which barely protruded from his face. 'Well, I would definitely say that it's best to approach this person from a loving place. You could try to encourage them without alienating them. It also depends on the person, and when you try, you would have to remember ultimately to have bitachon, to have trust in God, and that you really can't control other people or judge them –'

Rabbi Levy's eyes averted to Thomas, who appeared beside Isaac.

'Thomas, nice to see you again,' said Rabbi Levy, shaking Thomas's hand, 'Shabbat Shalom.'

'Shabbat Shalom,' replied Thomas, grinning.

'I see you've appeared with your teacher tonight. I hope you enjoyed the service this evening?'

'Oh, yes, it's great. It's so beautiful and stunning, just the architecture and the design.'

'It goes back over a century,' said Rabbi Levy. 'Would we have the honour of hosting you this Shabbat, or are you already taken?'

Isaac looked at Thomas, who was already opening his mouth to respond. He hadn't officially invited Thomas for dinner tonight. He kind of had forgotten, but he was going to bring him home afterwards anyway. He had mentioned to his mother earlier that he was going to attend the services tonight, and he couldn't imagine Thomas going anywhere else.

'Sure,' said Thomas.

'Fantastic,' said Rabbi Levy. 'It would be our pleasure. We shall be out in a few minutes.'

'OK,' said Thomas excitedly.

'Thank you so much, rabbi,' said Isaac, shaking hands with him again.

'Shabbat Shalom,' said Rabbi Levy.

'Shabbat Shalom,' said Isaac. He then turned to Thomas. 'Enjoy.'

'Thanks,' said Thomas. 'I shall see you soon. Tomorrow?'

'Yes,' said Isaac.

Good, Isaac thought while walking back home with his father. Thomas was now having Shabbat dinner with Rabbi Levy. He was sure that Rabbi Levy would share some essential details about Judaism and conversion with Thomas, and this would help Thomas develop a relationship with Rabbi Levy, who would, God-willing, supervise his conversion.

He was also wondering how he would incorporate Rabbi Levy's advice with regards to his friends. He had to approach them from a loving place and he had to encourage them, but how would he do so? He had already tried to figure out where they were coming from individually. Now, he had to encourage them to do things they had already done previously throughout most of their entire lives. How was he to do that? It seemed as though he had been annoying them. Was this already a lost cause? Was there still a chance that he could bring them back to living a religious life again? He felt that if he couldn't then he would feel alienated from his own best friends. Or was he wrong? Could he still have a relationship with them if they weren't religious?

Upon arriving home, he had put these confusing thoughts to rest. It was draining him of his mental strength. The table was set, and they began their meal. As Isaac took his portion of the various dishes, he turned to his sisters, who sat before him.

'Have you guys, by any chance, seen Ben at the supermarket?'

Ruth shook her head.

'No,' said Sarah, as she held a scoop of Israeli salad.

'Oh,' uttered Isaac under his breath as he looked down.

He figured there were a lot of things that he didn't like that he would just have to accept.

CHAPTER XVII

Isaac continued his daily sessions with Thomas throughout the following week. He would teach him at three o'clock for about an hour, sometimes more if they got sucked into a topic or just wanted to have a personal conversation. Isaac was now learning for several hours consecutively in the morning as before.

One Tuesday afternoon, after studying for three hours straight, Isaac decided he'd go buy some food for lunch at Gan Eaten.

Once there, he headed towards the produce section in the back, thinking he'd grab some fruit before getting some yoghurt. As he perused the open section, he caught sight of none other than Benjamin Jacobs stacking melons.

Filled with excitement, he quickly walked up to him. 'Ben!'

Benjamin turned around and smiled upon greeting him. 'Oh, hey! How are you, Isaac?'

'I'm well, thanks. How are you? I did not expect to see you here. I thought you'd stopped working here or something.'

'Oh, no. Actually, I went on holiday for a bit, but then I was out sick after that. Why? Did you come by here and not see me?'

'Yes,' said Isaac.

'Oh, you must've come when I was out, then. I came back yesterday.'

Isaac nodded. 'Right. Well, it's so good to see you.'

'Thank you, you as well,' said Benjamin. 'It's nice to have someone around here tell me that.'

'Right,' said Isaac, laughing. 'I meant to ask you – I know you had told me before that you were interested in learning about Judaism.'

As Isaac was saying these words, he could not believe that God had put him in this opportune situation right now.

'Yes,' said Benjamin, looking as though he were about to say something else, but he stopped to listen to what Isaac had to say.

'I wanted to ask if you would like me to teach you about Judaism?'

Benjamin grinned in pure joy and excitement. 'Oh, thank you, yes! I've been wanting to learn about my faith, but I didn't know where to start – I've never been to a yeshiva and wasn't sure how it works. I appreciate your offer!'

Isaac tried to hide his own excitement so as not to overwhelm Benjamin with fear – that was how excited he felt. 'Great! What's your number? I could teach you at my place.'

'Sure,' said Benjamin.

They exchanged contacts.

'What time and day work best for you?' asked Isaac.

'Sundays are best.'

'What time Sunday?'

'All day.'

'How about we do four thirty?'

Isaac figured a half-hour gap between his sessions with Thomas and Benjamin that day would give him enough time to mentally prepare.

'That sounds great,' said Benjamin.

'We could talk more about possibly other days later,' said Isaac.

'OK. So, I shall see you on Sunday, then?' said Benjamin.

'Yes,' said Isaac. 'Also, have you ever had a Shabbat meal?'

'No.'

'Would you like to come for a Shabbat dinner this Friday?'

'Yeah, I'm free then,' said Benjamin.

'Amazing. You're going to love it,' said Isaac.

'I'm sure I shall,' said Benjamin, still refraining from continuing to stock the melons.

'All right, well, I shall see you on Friday,' said Isaac.

'See you then. Thank you,' said Benjamin.

'My pleasure,' said Isaac, nodding and walking away. For a moment, he had forgotten the reason for which he had come to the supermarket. He had even forgotten that he was hungry. He was so excited to have met Benjamin again, and even more so to have scheduled his first lesson to teach him about Judaism, and now he had his contact information in case he'd disappear again.

CHAPTER XVIII

Isaac had a successful lesson with Thomas on Thursday afternoon, which would be his last before Shabbat. All that was left to look forward to was Shabbat with both Thomas and Benjamin as guests for dinner, and then Sunday after that, in which case Isaac would have sessions with Thomas and Benjamin. He found it amazing that it would be Benjamin's first Shabbat meal. He felt honoured that his family would be hosting it. He couldn't wait to introduce Thomas and Benjamin to each other, two students of his who were genuinely interested in learning about Judaism. He knew that even if they didn't become friends, they would be a good influence on each other. Isaac was so excited Thursday night after supper and he decided to go for a walk in the busy streets of Central London on the cool autumn night. He now felt as though he were living in alignment with his life's purpose, if he ever had one.

As he was walking down the pavement with his hands in his pockets, he looked from time to time through the windows of the various businesses to his right. There was some sort of restaurant when he caught sight of Eliezer. He halted, staring from outside.

It really was Eliezer. He was at an Indian restaurant. There was nothing about the interior that suggested that it was a kosher restaurant; there was no certificate of kashrut or rabbinical supervision posted on the window or walls, and he was eating at the table by the window with three other people Isaac had never seen before. There was one man and two women, and the man was not wearing a kippah. None of the men in the restaurant, from the waiters to the diners, was wearing a kippah. There was nothing Jewish about the scene, save for Eliezer's being Jewish by birth due to Isaac's knowledge.

Isaac stared at whatever Eliezer was eating. He guessed it was chicken tikka masala based on pictures he had seen, though he wasn't sure because he had never seen it before in real life. It did appear to be some sort of meat dish from the looks of it, and whatever cream-coloured beverage he was having looked as though it were dairy. Isaac felt sick.

Eliezer looked at Isaac, and for a second, it was as though Isaac's heart had forgotten how to beat. Isaac noticed the other man in the group was pointing at Isaac, seemingly laughing at the looks of Isaac. He had been standing there staring at them!

Eliezer looked a bit concerned as he waved, but Isaac was filled with embarrassment and walked away. As he got further away from the restaurant, his heart grew with fury.

Why was Eliezer eating at an Indian restaurant? Did he want to become a goy?

Eliezer's calling his name outside did not help; it only aroused more anger. He could feel his face flush. He must have been as red as a tomato. Whatever embarrassment he had felt just a few seconds ago had now been fully replaced by vexation; whatever joy and excitement inspired this walk had now been forgotten.

'Isaac!'

Isaac thought that Eliezer's call was a bit closer, but he marched on, approaching the street. Just before he put his foot on the zebra crossing, Eliezer yanked him by his shoulder, and due to his own mercy for his friend, he acquiesced and turned around, curious to know whatever justification or explanation he could have for him now.

'Isaac,' said Eliezer, catching his breath. He was outside without his coat in November; he had left it in the restaurant as he had rushed out of it to talk to him. 'How are you?'

'How am I?' yelled Isaac. 'What were you doing there?'

'Oh,' said Eliezer. Isaac couldn't believe, due to the surprise in Eliezer's tone, that he would've expected to steer the conversation in any other direction. How could he have expected Isaac not to address this? And why would he choose to ignore it? Was he pretending like Isaac was someone else? 'I was just spending time with some friends.'

'How could you?' asked Isaac, waiting to hear Eliezer's response.

Eliezer was still catching his breath. He shook his head; he seemed to have no answer.

'Goodbye, Eliezer.' Isaac set out to cross the street, but Eliezer put out his hand to stop him again.

'Wait – Isaac!' he said.

'What?'

'Wait,' Eliezer said under his breath.

Isaac laughed as Eliezer was still catching his breath. He looked at the Indian restaurant.

'Please don't be angry with me,' begged Eliezer, his voice beginning to sound fragile. 'Please.'

Isaac stepped back, thus removing Eliezer's hand from his shoulder.

'You've changed,' said Isaac, scowling at him. And with that, Isaac crossed the street with the crowd of other Londoners.

'Wait!' called Eliezer, reaching out his hand.

Isaac kept walking as Eliezer remained on the other side of the street.

'Isaac!' cried Eliezer.

Isaac made no gesture in acknowledgement; no passer-by could tell that he was the person whom Eliezer had been calling.

He took the next turning on the right to go to the nearest underground station; he had seen enough tonight. His leisurely walk had come to an end. His heart was pounding with anger. His friends had clearly changed. They were now unrecognisable to him; they were like new people. And what reason did he have to continue to talk to them or spend time with them? To long for the old days of how they used to be? To continue to be heartbroken by witnessing the people they had become?

If that was the way they wanted to be, so be it, thought Isaac. That was their choice. Being with them would bring no improvement, no good. He now only cared about the growth of Thomas and Benjamin, who were now his new friends. If this was the beginning of a new era, then he was to proceed with it.

With regards to Eliezer, Simon, and Ariel, they had clearly chosen different paths. He was not to associate with them anymore.

PART II

CHAPTER XIX

Ariel called that Sunday just a few minutes before Isaac's session with Thomas. Isaac wondered what his former friend wanted. He stood by his decision to no longer speak to his former friends; he did not call him back. He kept thinking about it until Thomas knocked on the front door, and he opened it, letting him in.

'Hey,' Thomas said, grinning. 'Wow, what a great Shabbat that was!'

Isaac was able to show him a smile, but as he and Thomas entered the living room, and Thomas took his seat at the dining table, Isaac could not stop thinking about his former friends and the anger he had towards them for abandoning their sacred heritage.

'Let's go over some of the laws of kashrut,' said Isaac, now going over the Jewish dietary laws. 'The commandment of kashrut is mentioned in the Chumash.'

Isaac paused, looking down.

'You're red,' observed Thomas, looking a bit serious, but still maintaining his usual cheery countenance.

'Yes, I'm very upset,' said Isaac. He couldn't stop thinking about his former friends, who had become non-observant. Meanwhile, here he was now with someone trying to join the religion and observe the commandments, and he wasn't even born Jewish. 'It's nice to see *someone* is interested in studying Torah.'

'What do you mean?' asked Thomas.

Isaac started pacing back and forth. He shook his head.

'You'd be surprised, Thomas. There are some people who don't have any care about what you want to learn right now.'

'I still have no idea what you're talking about,' said Thomas.

Isaac stopped pacing, now making eye contact with Thomas, as his chair was now angled towards him. He decided to stop the vagueness. 'I have friends, Thomas, who don't care about Judaism anymore. I have no idea why, but it makes me sick. It really hurts. I have a lot of contempt for them. They're not living good lives.'

Thomas stared at him. He blinked and took in a deep breath before responding after several seconds of silence. 'Isaac, didn't we learn about lashon hara?'

Isaac's eyes were wide open. He was stunned.

'Evil tongue – isn't that right? When someone talks bad about someone and says bad things about them – I am getting the phrase right, right?'

'Yes,' said Isaac, pausing before continuing, his jaw hanging for a little while, 'yes, that's what it's called.'

Isaac couldn't believe it. His own student corrected him during their third week into their sessions. Thomas was right; it was not good to speak negatively about his friends just to vent his frustration. He supposed that this was the result of teaching Thomas, his response to him. He also meant it as a sort of praise for Thomas, but seeing that Thomas wasn't going along with what he was saying, he carried on with the lesson.

CHAPTER XX

Isaac had a brilliant week of teaching. He was now teaching Thomas at three o'clock every day from Sunday through Thursday. Thomas was excelling in his studies and the books Isaac and Rabbi Levy had been recommending. Isaac was also teaching Benjamin Sunday through Thursday in the evenings right after supper, though Benjamin couldn't make it Thursday night during what was their first full week. Isaac and Benjamin had to have their sessions in Isaac's room as the other members of Isaac's family would, one by one, have supper at the dining table during that time.

It was the second Sunday that saw Isaac teaching both Thomas and Benjamin. At one o'clock, after a full morning of blissful studying and exciting planning, Isaac decided to grab food for lunch at Gan Eaten as he still had two hours before his lesson with Thomas. He was very much looking forward to his sessions with Thomas and Benjamin later that day.

He entered Gan Eaten and looked around the supermarket, wondering what he'd buy, as if he had never gone there before. There were some shoppers here and there, as was normal for a Sunday afternoon. It was when he reached the middle aisle that contained coffee and spices that he turned to the left and saw none other than Eliezer by the meat refrigerators against the wall of the supermarket. His back was turned towards him, and he appeared to be with some young woman.

Isaac froze, but not for long; his first instinct was to run out of sight, and that was what he went with. Why hadn't he gone to Kosher Garden instead?

Where exactly in the supermarket Isaac was marching to, he did not know, but apparently, he had suddenly decided to go to the dairy refrigerators by the produce section towards the back. He observed absent-mindedly the various flavours of yoghurt and ice cream, which he would not buy, as his heart moderated its rate after having been so high.

He took a deep breath, staring at his faint reflection on the cool refrigerator door that blew cold air onto his body. He was safe now.

'Isaac!'

He couldn't stop himself from jumping as he turned around, as Eliezer and his companion approached him, and he tried to give a wide grin.

'Isaac, how are you? I haven't seen you for so long! This is my friend, Margaret.'

His friend, whom he had recognised as being one of the people he had seen dine with him when he had spotted him that night in the Indian restaurant, grinned and said, 'Hi, nice to meet you. You can call me Marge.'

Clearly, if this young woman was Jewish, she was not so religious as she had been eating at a non-kosher restaurant, and since Isaac had seen her there alongside him, Isaac assigned blame to her for being a negative influence on him for having eaten there.

Isaac, looking at Eliezer whilst refraining from introducing himself to her, recovered from his shock and said, 'Yes, it has been a while.'

'What have you been up to?' Eliezer asked.

Isaac was confused. Why was he acting like that night by the Indian restaurant had never happened? he thought. He was also unaware of his intention to no longer speak to him. There was no point in sharing that, as it would only lead to greater conflicts and negative emotions, not to mention that it would embarrass him in front of his companion.

'The same as usual.'

'How have you been?' Eliezer asked, continuing with his tone of enthusiasm.

'Baruch Hashem,' replied Isaac, checking to see how Margaret would respond. Seeing that she now looked at Eliezer and him in confusion, he figured that she did not know it meant 'Thank God' or 'Very well' and that she was probably not Jewish.

There was a moment of silence that seemed to stretch as Isaac stared at the young adults before him, who in turn were doing nothing other than the same to him.

After their brief career as statues, Isaac said, 'Well, I've got to get going. It was nice seeing you.'

Eliezer and Margaret watched him go as Isaac waved goodbye to them.

'Bye,' said Margaret.

'Oh, OK,' said Eliezer, whose grin was now painted with confusion.

Isaac didn't know what he wanted now. He wandered around Gan Eaten like a lost child.

'Isaac,' came that dreadful voice again.

Isaac, who had just entered the adjacent aisle lined with tins of tomatoes (though he was not planning on having them for lunch), turned around and quietly sighed at the sight of Eliezer, but he now approached him with a low tone and privately.

'Isaac,' he said, 'what's the matter? Are you OK?'

Isaac swallowed. What was he to say? He thought he had ridden himself of this nuisance. He could not be more at odds emotionally with the speaker overhead playing Jewish dance music, unless, of course, dancing would scare him off, which it probably would, and he considered it for a moment, but said instead, 'Yeah. I'm fine.' He nodded.

Eliezer sighed. He smiled, and continued the conversation casually, clearly unable to read his sarcasm. 'Oh, great. I was just showing my friend what a kosher supermarket looks like.'

How could a kosher supermarket look so different from a regular supermarket? thought Isaac. It had food. Sure, maybe some prepared food would have labels on them in Hebrew, but what was the big deal? What a ridiculous idea for a hangout.

Before he could come up with a response, Miss Margaret appeared, emerging from behind the wall of shelves. Were these two to leech onto his life forever?

'Sorry, I've really got to go,' said Isaac.

'Oh, OK,' responded Eliezer, nodding and looking concerned for his urgency.

'See you later,' said Isaac, walking away without looking at Margaret again.

'See you,' said Eliezer, a hint of uncertainty still remaining in his voice.

Isaac kept to his word, and he left without buying anything. He'd purchase something at a nearby corner shop. Whilst walking out of the supermarket, he did not see Benjamin, and he was glad he hadn't seen him because he did not want Eliezer asking about him or the two of them meeting; he did not want Eliezer to be a negative influence on him, with his apathy towards Jewish practice possibly quenching Benjamin's interest in it, or Margaret's influence either, taking him to non-kosher restaurants and having him do other activities prohibited by Torah.

As he walked to the corner shop, he thought about all the non-kosher engagements this young woman could have been encouraging him to participate in. Although it made him cringe, he thought these mental explorations were necessary. Just what did he do whilst spending time with her, this new friend, as well as the other members of the group he had seen at the Indian restaurant – or any other friends he had?

He then had to stop; it was causing him too much mental pain. He was no longer friends with Eliezer and had thus absolved himself from being in connection to any of his many possible problems.

He now began to wonder how often he would be forced to interact with him or any of his former friends because they happened to be within proximity. He hoped never.

CHAPTER XXI

It turned out he didn't have to wait so long to receive the beginning of the answer. That Thursday night, Isaac went for a walk after supper through his neighbourhood of Golders Green. It was a little chilly that night. He then saw across the street Eliezer, Simon, and Ariel all emerging from a cinema.

At first, Isaac was struck with shock and joy, the latter of which had been the default reaction for the longest upon seeing them. All three of them were grinning. Isaac felt a certain warmth in his chest, in contrast to his cool hands, which were buried in his coat pockets.

They were walking down the street in the same direction as he was, albeit Isaac was doing so at a slower pace to observe them, seemingly spectating what had been his past life, or perhaps what could still be. It was like he was in a dream. He felt fearful for a moment that they would turn around and spot him, but the streets were fairly crowded, most dressed in black, including himself, and it was night. It would be very difficult to spot him if one of them were to turn around, at least within a few seconds.

He then started to feel a bit confused and a bit abandoned as their backs faced him. Why hadn't they invited him? Was he no longer considered part of The Team? They hadn't been notified of his desire to no longer speak to them, but it seemed as though they had already excluded him from the group on their own. How could they? he thought. How could they hang out – all three of them – without him? And what possible inappropriateness had been featured in the film they had just watched? He did not want to imagine.

His heart grew heavy in his warm coat on that chilly night. He was now as unimportant to them as was any of the pedestrians around him – whether Londoner, Welshman, or tourist, it did not matter. He apparently was no longer included in any of their hangouts.

He had no intention of contacting them, and this reinforced his decision. Their neglect of and disregard for him only supported his desire to no longer speak to them. He felt a pain in his chest, as though it were being inflated.

He heard them laugh. He then realised that he had missed the sound of their laughter. It was like some old, cheerful song. That familiar sound brought an overwhelming wave of nostalgia and pain to him. It was so delightful. He wondered what joke had just been shared and who had said it. Was it Ariel, who was talking now as he walked on the right side out of the three of them? He did not know; whatever laughter he would have tried to bring out of his friends he could not do; whatever love and belonging that could have still been harboured for them in secret was now overshadowed by pain and hurt. He could not bear it anymore. He shifted direction against his natural inclination of walking down that street; he took the next turning on the right.

CHAPTER XXII

Several weeks passed by, and Isaac hadn't seen his former friends since that Thursday night outside the cinema. He kept doing his lessons with Thomas and Benjamin. Benjamin had become a regular guest on Shabbat, as he couldn't keep it at home, and he was Jewish, thus, beholden to the commandments.

About a week before Hanukkah, Mrs Abrams confirmed that her brother, Mr Cohen, was coming to visit from Manchester with his family, and they would stay until Saturday night, which would be the seventh night of Hanukkah after it would have started on a Sunday night. Thus, they were coming on Sunday.

Isaac hadn't seen his cousins from Manchester for six years. Before his three-year stay in Israel, they were meant to visit them up north one summer, but it didn't end up working for Mrs Cohen. Nonetheless, Isaac was very excited to see them.

The Abrams family decorated the living room with Hanukkah-themed images and ornaments. The Cohens' trip was slightly delayed due to traffic. They arrived about a half hour before the afternoon service was to begin at synagogue.

The doorbell rang, and Mr and Mrs Cohen came in first with two of their children, Leah and Eliyahu.

Isaac's uncle and aunt asked Isaac about his well-being and current affairs after speaking to Mr and Mrs Abrams. Leah and Eliyahu gravitated towards his younger sisters.

Daniel, the oldest of the four Cohen children (which was obvious as he was quite tall), entered the entrance with Tikvah, the youngest, and they both pulled their suitcases in.

Isaac welcomed Daniel and Tikvah. As Mrs Abrams received Tikvah in the kitchen, Isaac asked Daniel, 'May I take your suitcase?'

'Sure,' said Daniel, who left it right where he was and walked past Isaac and into the living room, smiling and not wishing to speak another word to his cousin.

Isaac stood there in the entrance, a bit confused and surprised as he started to feel more like an assistant than a relative (who was a volunteer, he might add).

Isaac slowly dragged the heavy suitcase across the living room, looking to see if any of his relatives would have cared to speak another word to him. No one did, as the room was filled with conversation, though Mordechai did seem rather quiet as he stood near a corner by the windows with his arms crossed as he spoke with Leah and Eliyahu.

Isaac brought Daniel's suitcase to Mordechai's room where Daniel and Eliyahu would be staying.

Isaac returned to the living room, feeling a bit disconnected from everyone else as their conversations flourished whilst his silence did. He was a bit confused; Daniel was just a year younger than him. They would laugh and joke together whilst growing up, even if they hadn't seen each other so often. Why was he being so distant now? He had barely spoken to him upon seeing him when he had arrived. Had six years brought a sense of apathy? Had he heard that Isaac had studied in Israel at yeshiva for three years and was now contemptuous of that? His guessing games ended when he looked at the clock on the living room wall and saw that services were to begin in five minutes.

'I've got to go to synagogue,' he announced as he headed towards the coat rack in the entrance, where he grabbed his coat and walked quickly to the synagogue. Just seconds after he had arrived at his place of prayer, the service began.

Isaac had brought Thomas to some of the services to guide him on the order of prayers through first-hand experience. He now attended synagogue every Shabbat and many other services throughout the week. He was praying here now, and he sat in the row a couple of rows behind Isaac to his left. Isaac still hadn't taught Benjamin the order of prayers, nor had he brought him here during the week, but he had come to some of the Shabbat services. Benjamin's work timetable did make it a bit difficult to come and pray, as well as other activities he enjoyed filling his week with, and he was not present tonight. Isaac had hoped that he would have turned up for at least some of the Hanukkah services. It was a festival, after all.

Mr Abrams, Mordechai, Mr Cohen, Daniel, and Eliyahu eventually arrived. After the afternoon services, Rabbi Levy gave a talk about Hanukkah, and then the evening service began. After the evening service, Isaac turned around and saw that Thomas was still praying, but that wasn't the only thing he noticed; Eliezer, Simon, and Ariel were also there. They were standing by the doors of the sanctuary.

Isaac didn't have much time to think. His father and brother wished him a happy Hanukkah, which he did in exchange. The Cohens stood in the middle of their row looking very uncomfortable, wide-eyed as if they were aliens from outer space. Isaac wondered whether they went to synagogue often anymore.

Isaac really wanted to wish Thomas a happy Hanukkah, but he wanted to eliminate any chance of his former friends meeting him; they would not be a good influence on Thomas. He figured he would go around the front of the seating section and go up the other aisle and thus take the long way out of the synagogue; this way, he would avoid his former friends. If Thomas greeted him and his former friends saw, he would not introduce them to each other, and he would also not have to introduce his antisocial cousin to him, either. Thus, he left the synagogue straight away.

Back at home, the table was already set, and the women were chatting at the extended dining table draped in white tablecloth filled with blue Hanukkah-themed decorations – images of dreidels, menorahs, and jelly-filled doughnuts.

The other men came about fifteen minutes later after conversing in the synagogue and on the way home with each other and with other congregants. They all lit menorahs on the windowsill in the living room and sang Hanukkah songs before partaking in the meal. Isaac and Daniel still seemed to not be talking so much, which Isaac had no choice but to accept for the time being. Daniel was very much in conversation with Mr Abrams, Mr Cohen, and Mordechai. This was probably due in part to the fact that Isaac had rushed out of the synagogue so suddenly. The dinner brought some sort of improvement. Isaac sat next to Mordechai. Sarah sat opposite him. He mostly spoke with them throughout the course of the meal. His younger cousin Eliyahu sat to his left, and he proved to be quite friendly and cheerful.

The meal dragged on for quite a few hours. There was much eating, conversing, and the younger ones even broke out some board games. What had started as joy and excitement slowly turned into exhaustion about two and a half hours later, though the adults had a lot of catching up to do after not having seen each other for over six years.

Mr Abrams announced it was time to recite grace after meals even though everyone, particularly the younger children, could still eat all the jelly-filled doughnuts they wanted afterwards. He yawned as everyone else accepted the reality that this meal would at some point – *could* at some point – come to an end (Isaac, however, was ready for bed).

They recited grace after meals, and the conversation and eating continued.

Over half an hour later, Mr and Mrs Cohen announced their intention to retire, the first of the Cohens to do so. All of Isaac's siblings had already done so. As his parents had risen from their seats to go to bed after Mr and Mrs Cohen, he was inspired to do the same.

Isaac brought back his plate and silverware to the kitchen. Mr and Mrs Cohen retired to the guest room. Mr Abrams yawned again upon exiting the living room to go to his bedroom.

Isaac returned to the dining table to grab his glass and napkin.

'Isaac,' whispered Mrs Abrams, popping her head out of the kitchen, and beckoning him over.

Her intention not to be heard by the Cohen children was a success. All of the Cohen children were now joking at the dining table, and they were growing increasingly louder.

Isaac headed to the kitchen. He was nervous to know what secretive information his mother was about to convey. They stood at the centre of the kitchen, the kitchen light hanging above her, lighting up her pale face, in contrast to the darkness portrayed by the kitchen window behind her. Outside, it was pitch black. He looked at the clock on the microwave – it was half past ten!

'Isaac, can you please do me a favour? Could you please entertain your cousins while I go to sleep? I'm very tired. I feel awful leaving them alone there.'

'Sure,' Isaac acquiesced. He wasn't nearly as tired as his mother, and the main reason he had wanted to go to bed was not because of his fatigue but because of boredom. His cousins had a style of throwing jokes around the dining table that didn't appeal to him, and they seemed to have been sharpened, furnished, and manufactured with all of their intricacies by them and for them; he didn't understand half of the references, the inside jokes, or what the meaning was behind the strange sounds they were making.

'Thank you,' she said, embracing him and kissing him on the head. 'Goodnight.'

'You're welcome. Goodnight.'

Isaac returned to the table. Entertaining his cousins only required his physical presence; they seemed to be perfectly capable of amusing themselves. Their jokes had become at times vulgar, and he was a bit intimidated by the sudden banter, wondering if they would include him as the object of it next. He wouldn't want to continue volunteering to 'entertain' them if they would.

The talking grew louder, as did the laughter. The dinner seemed to continue forever.

Isaac was starting to wonder how such people could be related to him. Their behaviour was so much different from his and that of his siblings and parents, and he was starting to notice that Daniel, presumably the one to set the example due to his age, was leading them in this way through how he spoke and acted. He felt bad for poor little Eliyahu, who sat between Daniel and him on this side of the table, whose mind was being taught that this was a proper way to be.

Nothing shocked Isaac that night as what happened next. Daniel took one of the jelly-filled doughnuts, laughing clumsily as he had done so (his sisters, sitting opposite Daniel and Eliyahu, offering their support through laughter as his audience), and observed that some of the grape jelly oozed out of a hole in the side of the doughnut. He turned towards Eliyahu, pressing the doughnut upon his forehead, thus giving Eliyahu a tiny jelly horn.

Everyone burst out laughing except Isaac, Eliyahu included, even though he didn't know how ridiculous he looked thanks to his older brother. Isaac wondered whether he was dreaming.

After fifteen excruciating minutes later, Isaac had to excuse himself and he ended up staying in his bedroom, where Mordechai was sleeping on a mattress on the floor next to his bed. The light was on. His mother had asked him to entertain the guests, but her conditions had never explicitly excluded the possibility of any breaks. So, he decided to read from the Chumash.

Daniel stepped into the room. Isaac could hear the girls laugh in the living room; his job was not even close to over. It was now a half-hour to midnight.

'Hey,' said Daniel.

'Hi,' muttered Isaac.

'Nice room,' said Daniel, looking around with his hands in his pockets.

'Thanks,' mumbled Isaac, not taking his eyes off the book.

Daniel then stood next to him, looking down at the open book. He was towering above Isaac's head.

'What's that you're reading?'

'The Chumash.'

'Ah, the Five Books of Moses,' said Daniel, as if he were an expert on Torah.

'Yeah.'

'May I learn with you?'

Isaac froze as his eyes shot wide open. What did he just hear? He was in such shock that he had to confirm this. He looked up at Daniel and asked, 'What was that?'

'Can I learn some Chumash with you?'

'Yes,' said Isaac. He had no reservations about learning Torah with a fellow Jew; he could not have imagined such a request coming from Daniel due to his behaviour and also because of his coldness, but he was excited to learn with someone else. 'Let's go to the living room.'

Isaac turned off the light in his bedroom, allowing Mordechai to sleep soundly in the dark.

By now, all of Daniel's siblings had left the living room.

Isaac went straight into studying Chumash with his cousin on the sofa until well past midnight. Daniel then admitted that he was feeling tired, and Isaac was a bit too, so he closed the book.

'Thank you,' said Daniel.

'No, thank you,' said Isaac. 'That was so much fun.'

Daniel smiled as his tired eyes were shut due to their new sensitivity towards the brightness of all the lights in the living room.

Isaac had forgotten just how enjoyable studying Torah with a study partner was. He spent much of his time studying alone; his old friends from yeshiva weren't religious anymore (and he no longer talked to them), leaving him with no one else to learn with whom he knew in the neighbourhood; he taught Thomas and Benjamin, which he wouldn't give up for anything, but he was mainly the instructor in these relationships. He had no one else to learn with who was also observant.

'Are you all religious?' asked Isaac.

'I'd say we're mostly traditional at this point,' said Daniel, shrugging.

'Do you spend any time studying?'

'Torah? Not really,' Daniel admitted.

Isaac was stunned. When he had last been with Daniel, he had also been in Jewish school. He was glad to know that he still believed in Judaism and was – to a certain extent, at least – practising.

'We should study again tomorrow if you'd like,' suggested Isaac.

'Yeah, I'm here all week,' said Daniel, looking excited as well.

And with that, they wished each other a good night, and within an hour, Isaac's opinion of his cousin had reversed.

CHAPTER XXIII

Isaac was surprised to see his former friends the next day after the evening service. It was a Monday. He wondered what they were doing here. Thomas approached him to wish him a happy Hanukkah, which he returned. He made eye contact with Ariel, who was standing by the doors with Eliezer, which made Isaac jerk his head and avert his eyes. Simon was still praying and swaying to Isaac's surprise. He then saw that Ariel beckoned to him; it seemed as though his fears from last night were coming true tonight.

He instinctively looked away again, pretending as though he hadn't seen Ariel.

'Follow me,' said Isaac to Thomas, not wanting him to think he wanted to end the conversation with him so quickly on a holiday; they hadn't been able to catch up the night before.

So, he decided to stick to last night's strategy. He led Thomas around, up the other aisle, and towards the doors.

Eliezer, who was just several metres away by the other doors, called his name, but he pretended not to hear.

'Isaac, he's calling you,' Thomas said from behind, even turning to Eliezer to acknowledge him.

But Isaac didn't and, as they passed through the entrance of the synagogue, Isaac still ignored Thomas when he asked, 'Who is he?' until they reached outside.

'That was Eliezer,' said Isaac, now walking adjacent to Thomas on the pavement.

'Do you know him?' asked Thomas.

'Yes.'

'What about the guys who were standing next to him?'

'Yes.'

'Who are they?'

'Ari and Simon.'

'How do you know them?' asked Thomas, whose tone was mixed with intrigue and confusion.

'Thomas, that does not matter. I would just advise you not to talk to them,' said Isaac breathlessly and looking Thomas in the eye. 'You don't want to associate yourself with them. They're not the best company.'

'Why?'

'Just take my word for it.'

Over the next several days, Isaac would study Chumash with Daniel, which proved to be such a pleasant experience. He also grew closer to his other cousins. He would joke around with them in the living room, and he would play games with them. He was starting to grow very fond of them, and he took a particular liking to Daniel. He appreciated that Daniel was very insistent to keep learning with him. They would learn together before Isaac's session with Benjamin in the evenings at seven o'clock, and sometimes afterwards as well if they both still had the energy.

Shabbat came, and Benjamin spent it with Rabbi Levy, which was very convenient for Mrs Abrams, as her hands were beyond full with the Cohens. Saturday night came, which brought with it the inevitable bidding farewell to the Cohens.

During that night, as the rest of the family conversed in the living room shortly before the Cohens departed, Isaac spoke with Daniel in his bedroom, where he was studying Chumash with Daniel at his desk.

'You know, I had a very different impression of you when you first came,' said Isaac.

'Really?' asked Daniel.

'Yes,' admitted Isaac. 'I took you to be…,' he paused, wondering what words he could use to remain honest yet tactful, 'reserved, but you've really opened up.'

'That's the first time I've ever heard that,' remarked Daniel, 'and I apologise if I've come across as cold.'

'That's all right,' said Isaac.

'I really wish I could stay longer. It's really been fun.'

'Yes, it has,' said Isaac.

'I hope to see you again soon,' said Daniel.

'Me too,' said Isaac.

Later that night, the Cohens were in the entrance with their luggage on their way out. Isaac said goodbye to his cousins. Then, they began their trip back home up north.

Isaac thought about it, and he regretted that all of his instruction to Thomas and Benjamin had been saturated with facts and details, but little emotion and fun. Yes, they were excited students, and they both asked engaging questions, but where was the fun? Judaism is fun!

He spent the whole week celebrating Hanukkah with his family. He thought now was a great time to have fun with his students. He could host a party Sunday night, on the eighth and final night of Hanukkah, for his family, Thomas, and Benjamin. He shared this idea with his mother, who hesitated a little at first – it had been a long week of hosting – but acquiesced as it was the final night of Hanukkah tomorrow. Thomas and Benjamin both agreed to join in the Hanukkah celebration.

So, they all kept the decorations in the living room, did a little cleaning the next day, and Isaac was off to the afternoon service of Hanukkah with Mr Abrams and Mordechai. He had invited Benjamin to come to the services, which he did, and Thomas was there too, naturally. For whatever reason, Eliezer, Simon, and Ariel were also here tonight. Why they seemed to only appear when Isaac no longer wished to speak to them, Isaac did not know.

Isaac beckoned Benjamin over upon seeing him enter the sanctuary so that he could pray next to him and guide him throughout the services. After services, he did not have to avoid his former friends. They had already left. He, Mr Abrams, Mordechai, Thomas, and Benjamin walked home together, filled with cheerful conversation during that chilly December night.

The Hanukkah party was off to a great start. They lit the menorahs on the windowsill, except for Thomas and Benjamin, who had to light where they would be sleeping tonight, which was at their homes, and they sang songs. Everyone wore festive, colourful clothing. They had a nice dinner, substantial with beef, latkes, knish, and coleslaw. Later, they played music and some board games. They shared words of Torah, and later they drank wine and danced. Isaac was full of bliss. He was so happy to celebrate with Thomas and Benjamin. By now, Thomas and Benjamin had become friendly with each other. Thomas even spoke with Mordechai more. Thomas and Benjamin also looked so happy. Isaac was glad to see that his mission of sharing the joy of being Jewish with them had been such an enormous success. He wondered how this could have been any better.

He was dancing with Benjamin, Thomas, and Mordechai when, as the rest of his family sat at the dining table and watched, Isaac noticed someone waving outside. He broke from the dancing group and inched closer to the window, peering through amidst the reflection of lights from the menorahs.

It was Simon! He was outside waving at him, smiling. What was he doing here?

He wasn't sure whether it was due to the effect of the drinking and the music, but even though he was disappointed to see him, as was usually the case now, a part of him also felt a little happy to see him.

'I've got it,' said Mordechai, who had also been looking through the window.

Isaac froze.

'Hey!' he heard Simon exclaim from the entrance.

Isaac wanted to end the party then and there. Whatever way he felt, he certainly did not want his former friends intermingling with his new ones.

Simon emerged from the dim entrance and entered the living room, followed by Mordechai.

'Isaac!' yelled Simon, going up to him to embrace him tightly.

Thomas and Benjamin stopped dancing and stared at Simon.

Isaac could feel the awkwardness in the room. He had told both Thomas and Benjamin to stay away from his former friends. Indeed, he had spoken negatively about them in order to ensure that they would follow his suggestion. Now, they were following his advice but were perplexed as to why Isaac suddenly wasn't and had, apparently, invited one of the very people he had instructed to avoid.

'Happy Hanukkah,' said Simon, grinning with his jaw hanging. 'I was walking by and saw the party. I figured I had to come by.'

Isaac only smiled. Mordechai had to have caught the discomfort Isaac had been feeling. He stepped forward and said, 'Simon, great to see you! How have you been?'

As the two of them engaged in conversation, Isaac went over to his immobile students and said, 'OK, guys. I think we shall call it a night. I'm so glad you guys came, but I'm starting to feel pretty tired.'

It was only half past eight, and although he would've rather told Simon to leave and to keep partying, he knew that would be inappropriate. After everything that had happened between them, Isaac was unwilling to embarrass him like that.

Sarah, upon hearing this, then turned off the music.

'Aw, what happened? I missed the party?' said Simon.

'Sorry,' said Mordechai.

Mr and Mrs Abrams greeted Simon and asked about his well-being.

Isaac made sure to dismiss Thomas and Benjamin before dismissing Simon. Fortunately, his parents kept Simon in conversation whilst he ushered Thomas and Benjamin out of the house so they wouldn't meet. After Mordechai had spoken to him, he knew Simon wouldn't leave until he asked him to, or over an hour after disappearing into his bedroom after he would have finally got the picture.

'Isaac, I haven't seen you in so long!' said Simon.

'I know,' said Issac, pretending to look and sound ten times as tired as he was.

'How have you been?' asked Simon.

'Good, just tired. Sorry, I think I shall go to sleep now,' said Isaac, squinting.

'Oh, OK,' said Simon, now concerned to let Isaac get enough sleep.

Isaac did notice that Simon seemed to look a bit disappointed due to being unable to converse with him. It seemed that though Isaac was no longer invited to outings, Simon did want to talk to him.

Isaac squinted as he stumbled his way to the front door, looking as though he were sleepwalking in order to maintain the appearance of being extremely fatigued, where he finally dismissed Simon. Simon was the primary source of the end of his once blissful party, which had so suddenly been cut short.

CHAPTER XXIV

After Hanukkah passed, Isaac resumed his normal teaching routine with his sessions with Thomas and Benjamin, which he had done throughout Hanukkah. New Year's Eve came, and though this was never so much of a big deal for Isaac as the Jewish New Year was on Rosh Hashanah, he still liked to reflect on the year and keep track of his goals and his progress.

He thought a lot about Hanukkah and the immense joy he had. He thought a lot about Daniel, how he had become less observant though still committed to being Jewish and learning Torah. He thought about how open he was to studying Torah, and he wondered how many Daniels there were in his life – Jews who were still loyal to Judaism but who had become less observant than before and who hadn't yet become an Eliezer, Simon, or Ariel. Maybe Isaac had caught Daniel at the right time, and he, as his family, would have continued to become more and more distant from Judaism and had he met Daniel years later, he would have become indifferent towards Judaism to the point where he wouldn't have wanted to study Torah with him.

After much reflection, Isaac was no longer inclined to win Jews over to living an observant life but committed now to maintaining the loyalty that Jews already observant in his life had towards Judaism through Torah study and social events. He thought of all the Jews he was close to who fit this category. There was Benjamin, of course, Thomas, who was in the process of conversion, Daniel, and his friends from yeshiva in Israel. He could think of no one else. Eliezer, Simon, and Ariel had already shown their lack of interest in reconnecting to Judaism, despite their random attendance in synagogue services.

In Israel, Isaac had four friends who had also been his study partners whilst in yeshiva: Shlomo, Moshe, Asher, and Adam. He had kept in contact with them through Facebook, which was new and had been growing in popularity. It would be difficult to study with them through Facebook messaging, and international calls were expensive. Moshe lived in Canada, and Shlomo and Asher lived in the United States, but he remembered that Adam lived in London. Nearby, in fact, in Hendon. Thank God, he thought, there was someone else he could connect with!

Apart from that, whilst having lunch after his morning study session, he also thought of Pinchas, who was his friend from Jewish primary school. They had hung out and studied together during the first couple of summers going into Jewish secondary school, but Isaac had grown closer to his former friends, and they had eventually stopped talking. He hadn't been in contact with him since well before going to study in Israel.

He was going to take a chance. These were the only other two Jews he could think of to study Torah with, and he would wait until the Second of January to call them and make plans to study together, in case they were too preoccupied with plans on New Year's Day.

So, on the second day after the ushering in of the year 2009, Isaac called Daniel, asking him whether he would be open to studying over the phone, to which Daniel enthusiastically agreed. They agreed to study Chumash together, and they would do so at nine o'clock at night for an hour, which gave Isaac something to eagerly look forward to after supper and after his session with Benjamin. They would study together from Sunday through Thursday.

Next, he called Adam.

'Hello?' answered Adam.

'Hi, Adam. It's Isaac.'

'Isaac Abrams?'

'Yes.'

'Oh, hey! How have you been?' asked Adam.

'Great,' said Isaac. 'I remembered that you live near me in London. I was wondering whether you'd like to learn together sometime.'

'Oh, yes, of course,' answered his former study partner. 'I think Sundays work best for me, in the morning.'

'Does ten o'clock sound good?'

'Sounds great,' said Isaac, before catching up with him.

So, they were set to learn Mishnah Berurah on Sunday mornings.

Last but not least, he only had to call Pinchas, but he had used an old mobile phone when he used to be in contact with him, and he was not listed as one of his eighteen friends on Facebook.

He searched through the several papers in his desk drawer and came across a small, old notebook where he had written some contact information. He found Pinchas's mobile number but not his home number. He dialled it, hoping it would still be the number he used because, if not, there would be no hope of keeping in touch with him. He didn't attend his synagogue and he had never been to his place before.

'Hello?' spoke Pinchas.

'Hello!' exclaimed Isaac, overjoyed to hear it was him.

'Who is this?'

'It's Isaac! Do you remember me? Isaac Abrams.'

'Oh, hi, Isaac. How have you been?'

'Good, I just wanted to know whether you would be interested in learning Torah together sometime.'

'Oh, that sounds exciting. When are you available?'

'When are you available?' asked Isaac.

There was a short pause.

'How about Wednesday at eight in the evening?'

'Wednesday at eight works great,' said Isaac.

So, they decided to learn the Gemara on Shabbat on Wednesdays at Isaac's place.

That Sunday morning was the first study session with Adam in the living room, that Sunday night was the first session with Daniel over the phone, and that Wednesday night was the first session with Pinchas in his room. These sessions went remarkably well.

Isaac was so pleased. He really had so much fun with his students and his study partners. To be with Adam again was like bringing back to existence a piece of his experience in Israel, and he felt more whole. He was off to such a splendid start this new secular year, and for once in his life, he had never felt so in tune with his mission in life.

CHAPTER XXV

The first full week went by with Isaac's new timetable, including all of the sessions with his students and his study partners. This new secular year was off to a great start. Isaac was full of bliss.

It was after supper one Tuesday and Isaac went to the kitchen to grab a clementine as a snack and thus took a short break from his personal studying. He heard the front door open, but all the members of his family were there and he had no upcoming session any time soon.

He kept his ears open for any familiar voice, but after some silence, he forgot about the sound of the door opening and ate some more fruit.

Someone was pulling one of the chairs by the dining table.

'How have you been?' he heard Mrs Abrams ask.

'I've been very well, thank you,' said a strangely familiar voice.

'You've come by yourself,' spoke Mr Abrams by the dining table. 'Is everything all right?'

'Yes, yes, thank you.'

Isaac paused. He drew closer to the door to the kitchen. He could only guess one person to be the source of this voice, but how could it be her?

Her image was blocked by the wall. He was too hesitant to check and see, worried she might see him.

'Would you like something to drink?' offered Mr Abrams.

'No, no, thank you,' she returned. 'That's very kind.'

The woman cleared her throat. Mr and Mrs Abrams were just listening quietly.

'I've come to tell you that after long and careful consideration, I have arrived at a decision. I'm not going to keep pretending anymore. I know very well that the reason why there has been so much distance and conflict between our families is because of my not being Jewish. I do not wish to be a source of conflict between brothers. For the longest time, I had been blissfully ignorant about this, but after many talks and overheard slights, I have come to figure out that my not being Jewish was the source of the conflict. I've lived with this guilt for many years, knowing that I could not change anything as I am not Jewish, but whilst simultaneously knowing that in fact, I can change the situation. I have no pleasure in the separation of our families or intention for it to go on any longer, and so therefore, I have decided that I and our kids shall convert to Judaism.'

Isaac couldn't swallow. Although he was ninety-nine per cent sure who she was, he had to confirm it himself. He peeped into the living room, moving his head to the side for less than two seconds out of the opening and back into the kitchen, where he remained standing, frozen in shock. Indeed, it was his aunt, Mrs Abrams, sitting opposite his parents at the dining table.

Mrs Abrams sighed.

'Eliza, is this something you're sure you want to do?'

'Yes, yes, absolutely,' said his aunt.

'But do you know enough about Judaism?' asked Mrs Abrams.

'No, but I'm willing to learn,' she responded.

Mr and Mrs Abrams thought for a few seconds and then Mr Abrams asked, 'And this is something the kids want to do as well?'

'Yes, we've spoken about this,' said Mrs Abrams. 'My husband doesn't know. I had hinted to it, but he didn't seem quite on board.'

'But what good shall it do if he's only going to get upset about it?' asked Mr Abrams.

'What?' asked Mrs Abrams, sounding confused and disappointed.

Isaac couldn't believe it. He thought he was really dreaming. He started trembling as he stood alone in the kitchen, listening to the conversation. His aunt wanted to convert to Judaism? His cousins from his father's side of the family wanted to convert to Judaism? He had barely seen his uncle, aunt, and cousins. And now he was to have them as Jewish in the family? He wanted to jump in excitement. He couldn't stop thinking about the prospect of their conversion to Judaism.

'Eliza,' began Mr Abrams, 'I don't have any negative feelings towards you, but I do recognise that if this is indeed something you'd like to do, and it's to make things better, but my brother seems against it, how would it help?'

Mrs Abrams didn't speak for a moment.

Isaac's heart was beating heavily in his chest. He couldn't believe that his father would be discouraging her from doing this. He wanted to speak.

'But,' she began, 'I do want this. The kids want this. We all want this.'

'Who shall teach you about Judaism and everything when –,' began Isaac's mother, before Isaac came into the living room and interrupted her.

'I can teach you.'

Everyone turned to look at Isaac. Isaac's aunt smiled at him with her moist eyes. They had not seen each other in years. Isaac's parents were sitting with their arms crossed, sighing.

'Would you?' asked his aunt.

'I would be happy to,' said Isaac, realising then how packed his timetable was about to be.

'Well, if you want to,' said his mother.

'Thank you so much,' said his aunt.

'What day and time work for you?' asked Isaac.

Mr and Mrs Abrams sat mostly in silence again, only watching and listening to the dialogue.

'I would assume that learning more often would make the conversion go by more quickly, right?'

'It can take many months,' said Mr Abrams, 'up to a year, or even more.'

'We can learn as often as you can,' said Isaac.

Mrs Abrams looked down at the wooden table and said, 'OK. So, let's start with Monday through Friday at six. How does that sound?'

'I can do Monday through Thursday at six because Friday night is the Sabbath. How does that sound?'

'Great,' said his aunt. 'And where shall we learn?'

'Could we learn here?' asked Isaac, looking at his parents.

Mr Abrams nodded.

'Sure,' said his mother.

'Fantastic,' said Isaac, grinning.

'Wow, thank you all so much,' said Mrs Abrams. 'Well, I've got to get going,' she said, getting up on her feet. 'I do appreciate this.'

So, she headed towards the entrance, and Mr Abrams followed her to escort her to the front door.

Isaac then realised that he would have one hour of a break at eight o'clock between seven o'clock and ten o'clock in the evenings in which he'd be learning with or teaching people, except for Wednesdays, since he would be using that time to learn with Pinchas, but he could always have an early supper at five o'clock or a late one at ten o'clock. He didn't mind; learning and teaching Torah were much more important to him, and he could tolerate an early or late supper once a week.

After she had left, Isaac didn't hear his parents utter a single word about her or the encounter. They were mostly quiet throughout the rest of that night. He lingered near the kitchen and dining room, expecting one of them to voice an opinion, positive or negative, about his plans or behaviour, but they didn't mention a single word. It was as though she had never appeared.

CHAPTER XXVI

Isaac's aunt confirmed the next day by phone that she and her children would be able to start that day. After one hour of personal study that morning, apart from his other sessions, he devoted all his free time to preparing the lesson for four.

It was during these preparations and revising them at his desk in his bedroom when Mrs Abrams entered the room where the door was open and said, 'Isaac, Elizabeth and the kids are here.'

So, Isaac stood and greeted his aunt and cousins in the living room. They were smiling – the kind of smile that was worn by those who were committed to growth. His cousins were so much taller. They all took a seat at the dining table, except for Isaac, who taught whilst standing, as was usual.

Isaac took a moment to admire these relatives whom he hadn't seen in years.

'I actually mentioned to David that I was coming,' said Mrs Abrams. 'He asked where I and the kids were going, naturally, and so, I told him.'

'How did he react?' asked Isaac.

'He barely did,' she said. 'So, I then offered him to come with us, but he refused.'

Isaac nodded.

What this conflict was between the families, Isaac did not know. Apparently, a lot of it had to do with his uncle having married a non-Jew, based on what his aunt had mentioned at the dining table yesterday. He always had the feeling that it was between his father and his brother, Isaac's uncle. They were the brothers in these two couples. This reason regarding his aunt's identity supported that feeling, but whether there were other factors at play as well, he was unaware.

He looked into the eyes of his three cousins. Before he would start his lesson, he wanted to get to know them a little more. They were his family, after all, yet he felt so disconnected from them.

'How old are you now?' he asked them.

The youngest girl, named Catherine, spoke first. 'Thirteen.'

'Sixteen,' said Alice, the middle child.

'Nineteen,' said Sam.

Throughout his entire life, Isaac had grown up somewhat estranged from this side of his family. He had seen them on several occasions whilst growing up, but these occasions had become rarer and rarer in frequency, and when the last time he had seen his cousins was, he could not remember.

He saw the eagerness to learn in their eyes, causing his very own to become moist. He had always known his aunt and his cousins weren't Jewish, and here they were, determined to convert. His heart was filled with love, admiration, and inspiration. He was on the verge of crying. He had to break eye contact by looking at the floor, then pacing around, and he then began his lesson. He was successful in refraining from producing tears before them.

He was determined to see that Thomas, his aunt, and his cousins would convert.

CHAPTER XXVII

The next day, Isaac headed to Yehuda's Judaica. He wanted to purchase a new book on character development that was published by a rabbi whose writings he admired and was inspired by. He opened the door to the shop where he had been countless times.

Inside was spotless, as always. Yehuda always cleaned and maintained it very well. Every item that he had to sell was always in its right place, and his son Shmuel was the same way. He saw that Yehuda wasn't in today.

After going down the first aisle (he liked to admire books he knew were there as well as new releases), he saw Mordechai browsing through the shelves.

'What brings you here?' asked Isaac.

'I've been meaning to learn Gemara, but I'm not quite sure which one. I also haven't got someone to study with.'

'I can study with you,' said Isaac. Up until now, he didn't know why he hadn't thought of Mordechai in his list of Jews whom he wanted to maintain within Judaism. How could he have forgotten his own household?

'Would you?'

'Of course!'

'Great, then. Have you got any suggestions?'

They looked through the glimmering titles.

'How about Yoma?' asked Mordechai, pulling it out of the shelf and flipping through the pages.

'Sounds excellent,' said Isaac.

'Amazing,' said Mordechai, looking down at the book in his arms, and that was when Shmuel, grinning, approached from the other side of the aisle.

'Shalom,' said Shmuel, his brown dreadlocks moving as he walked.

'Shalom,' responded Isaac and Mordechai.

'How can I help you?' asked Shmuel, the lights of the shop reflecting on his large, round spectacles, his blue eyes hidden behind the glare.

'I think we've found what we want,' said Mordechai, closing the book and making eye contact with Shmuel.

'Oh, wonderful,' said Shmuel, 'and how have you been? It's good to see you.'

'Good, thank God,' said Mordechai. 'Isaac and I are going to study together. I'm very excited. You know, Isaac has become a teacher.'

'Have you?' asked Shmuel.

Isaac smiled. 'Sort of.'

'He's been teaching a future convert and a baal teshuva,' said Mordechai, the last two words meaning a non-religious Jew who had become religious. 'He's also learning with his own study partners, too.'

Clearly, Mordechai had not heard about his new sessions with their aunt and cousins, but Isaac was too embarrassed to mention it.

'Wow, amazing, and how have you been able to work while doing all that?' asked Shmuel. 'Are you working?'

'No,' answered Isaac, thus recalling an old issue of his.

'Why don't you become a rabbi and teach?' asked Shmuel.

Isaac shrugged. 'Well, I,' he began, but he didn't know quite what to say.

'That's a good idea,' said Mordechai. 'Why don't you?'

The truth was, Isaac had never thought about it. He had never heard of a shortage of rabbis who could teach in London, but he had never thought of becoming a rabbi and teaching Torah as a profession.

'You should,' said Shmuel.

They both encouraged him to do so some more and upon exiting the shop (he had to go back in shortly after having come out as he had forgotten to purchase the book he had come to buy), all he could think about was becoming a rabbi and teaching at a yeshiva. He started to feel very excited. This could very well be the answer to his questions – a way to earn money which was connected to his purpose in life! And then he thought, why hadn't he thought of that sooner?

CHAPTER XXVIII

The next week included the full timetable with all of Isaac's students and study partners: Thomas, Benjamin, Adam, Pinchas, Mordechai, his aunt, his three cousins from his father's side, and Daniel. The beginning of the week was full of bliss and excitement. By now, he had gained so much experience that teaching was barely intimidating or nerve-wracking. However, after his last session on Thursday, which was with Daniel over the phone and ended at five past ten at night, he had a headache and was very fatigued.

'I don't know what's going on,' he said at the dining table, where he and Sarah were having soup for supper. 'I'm not sure if I am coming down with something. I've had this headache since around noon. I'm so tired and I haven't got any energy. I don't know if I would be able to do this every week.'

Sarah asked Isaac what his timetable was like. After he warned her of its excessive details, she insisted on knowing, and he shared with her every student or study partner and his time slot throughout the week.

He was starting to feel rather demoralised. Didn't he enjoy teaching and learning Torah? Why was he feeling so low? How was he going to keep teaching everyone and growing through learning? How was he to teach at a yeshiva if it was clearly so mentally draining for him? Was he incapable of doing so? He admitted to himself that he had had little time for independent study this week, maybe an hour a day if he had managed to find the time, due to all the lesson preparations on top of his lessons and study sessions.

'You're burnt out,' observed Sarah, looking at him over her emptied bowl. 'Maybe you should cut down on some of your lessons. You could do Sunday through Wednesday instead of Thursday.'

This brought Isaac no relief. He was determined to see that Thomas and his aunt and cousins would convert, and every day that he would refuse to teach them would probably delay their conversion longer. He also didn't want to abandon any of the sessions with his study partners.

'I don't know,' he said. 'I want to teach them as much as I can.'

'But look at yourself,' she said. 'You look very exhausted. It's nice you want to teach, but you wouldn't have any energy left if you work yourself to exhaustion. What difference does it make if you teach four days a week instead of five? Maybe later, with more experience, you would be able to teach more.'

'I think you're right,' said Isaac after thinking about it.

So, they conversed a bit more, changing the subject of conversation, which Isaac thought was quite nice, as they didn't get a chance to speak and eat together so often outside of Shabbat. She recited grace after meals, rose, and took her bowl and utensils to the kitchen.

Isaac finished his supper. He recited grace after meals and did as Sarah had done.

Upon reflection of his timetable after having returned to his bedroom, he concluded that he did need to modify his timetable. He planned to have Thursdays off, thus no longer teaching Thomas, Benjamin, his aunt, or his cousins that day, but he would still learn with Daniel over the phone Thursday night. If he thought that he could handle another session on Thursdays, or if even phoning Daniel would be too much, then he would adjust as necessary. Otherwise, seeing that this was already a major shift, he did not feel the need to make any more changes. He would do so later if there was a need.

CHAPTER XXIX

That Sunday was the first day after Isaac's amendment to his timetable. Isaac and his aunt had agreed that they would do lessons on Sunday as well, which meant that he would teach his aunt and cousins from Sunday through Wednesday. He was feeling well-energised when his session with his aunt and cousins was about to start, though he would really have to see how he felt Wednesday or Thursday. Only his cousins would be attending today as his aunt had other engagements, so they took the tube to his place at Golders Green.

The session went rather well. His cousins asked lots of questions, more so than they would in their mother's presence. Isaac was starting to fantasise about teaching them separately for the purpose of their increased engagement, but he had to remember his new commitment to spending less time teaching for his well-being. Nonetheless, he was glad to see that they were engaging more.

After the session, which was extended as they spent time talking (they were cousins, after all), Isaac's cousins then rose from their seats and headed towards the entrance.

As Alice and Catherine stood on the front steps outside, Isaac and Sam lingered in the entrance.

'How is your father?' asked Isaac, having never enquired of him since teaching his aunt and his cousins. He felt freer to do so as his parents were nowhere around to hear.

'Oh, he's great, thanks,' said Sam, putting his hands into the pockets of his blue jacket as he looked down pensively. He sighed, and said, 'You know, something tells me he would've liked this, maybe even liked to have seen his brother again.'

'Why? You think so?' asked Isaac.

Seeing that the girls were outside conversing, Sam felt more comfortable speaking frankly about his father.

'He didn't want to come, Isaac, and he feels overshadowed.'

'How so?' asked Isaac.

Sam sighed again.

'I don't know. We haven't really spoken about it. This is what I'm concluding out of everything I've heard. All I know is that it seems like he's always felt like your father is superior to him – or maybe, others have made him feel he was superior, or both. I'm not quite sure. You'd honestly have to ask him.'

'All right,' said Isaac, feeling more confused than before as he held onto the front door.

'Anyways, thank you and have a good night,' said Sam.

They set off on the cold January night.

Isaac closed the front door. He wasn't quite sure what to make of his uncle. He knew he wasn't religious, and apparently, there was a possibility of him returning to religious life, and he had already established his purpose in life to help Jews around him who were secular and were interested in Judaism to return. However, his uncle was a grown man. He could make his own decisions and, should he wish to learn, he needed only to contact him. And with that, he put the matter aside.

CHAPTER XXX

Isaac mentioned his aunt and cousins' intention to convert, and that he was teaching them, to Rabbi Levy, and Rabbi Levy said that he would love to be their sponsor. Because they lived in Sutton, in South London, they wouldn't be able to walk to Rabbi Levy's synagogue, so they would have to find a synagogue much closer.

Isaac introduced his aunt and cousins to Rabbi Levy after the evening service the day after Sam had spoken to him about his father in the entrance. Isaac mentioned that she was his uncle's wife. Rabbi Levy seemed to have a very good impression of them and seemed to enjoy meeting them.

After their lesson that day, Isaac spoke with his aunt in the entrance as his cousins waited outside.

'Isaac,' she said, lowering her voice as they neared the front door, 'I thought I should mention to you my husband is interested in taking lessons with you.'

Isaac's head jerked back. He had difficulty believing his ears. 'He is?'

'Yes.'

Isaac wondered what had changed his uncle's mind.

'But he's intimidated,' she said. As Isaac was unaware of what to say next, she continued, 'He's always had a rocky relationship with his brother. I am part of the reason why,' she lowered her head as she spoke these last few words, then raised it again. 'He's quite intimidated to come here for lessons.'

Isaac thought about it. It would be difficult to take the train to Sutton every day for their lessons, considering how packed his timetable was and how exhausting the travelling would be on top of that. Nonetheless, it was quite promising and exciting that he had indicated interest.

'I shall think about it,' said Isaac, and then he said just as the idea came to his head, 'I know! We could call him while I'm giving lessons here!'

Mrs Abrams nodded. 'Great.'

'We shall just have to hide that we're calling him,' he said.

'Right,' she agreed.

He saw that she was gesturing towards the doorway, when he said, 'I'm just curious: what was it that made him interested?'

'I don't know; I can't say, but we've all been very excited about what we're learning, especially the kids; they feel as though they're connecting to their heritage. At home, we try to keep Shabbat the best way we can. Sam's been going to synagogue. He's been joining us on Shabbat, so I guess he's been drawn in. I can see he's interested, though. It would be great if he could become observant with us.'

'Wow, great,' said Isaac, his jaw hanging as he absorbed all this information in awe.

'All right, well, thank you so much for everything,' she said.

'You're welcome, have a good night,' said Isaac.

And so, his aunt and cousins descended the front steps. He stood there watching, his heart full of admiration and inspiration, as his relatives and students travelled on the road to becoming Jewish. He started picturing them as being Jewish already.

CHAPTER XXXI

Isaac had thought about his conversation with Shmuel and Mordechai at Yehuda's Judaica and Shmuel's thoughts about him becoming a rabbi to teach. He decided that he would go to Israel to study at a rabbinical school to receive his ordination to teach – a plan that was fully supported by Rabbi Levy and his parents. He felt a huge amount of relief after having made this decision. He now felt that his life had direction and meaning.

However, he did not want to go to Israel so quickly. He still had work to do in England. He wanted to continue studying with his study partners (he worried that leaving the country so soon after having established these connections would be not only neglectful but painful), and he also felt the obligation to keep teaching his students. He was still determined to see that Thomas, his aunt, and his cousins convert.

Wednesday of that same week with the discussions with his aunt and Sam regarding his uncle, Sam called Isaac, indicating that his mother was too busy with work that day and his sisters occupied with school.

'I would love to come,' explained Sam on the phone, 'but I'm honestly so tired. I don't think I'd be able to take the tube to your place tonight.'

'That's OK; I can take the train to your place,' Isaac replied instantly.

Sam paused for a bit. 'Could you?'

'Yeah, sure,' said Isaac.

Isaac heard in Sam's voice his willingness to learn and wanted to take advantage of that. He would call Benjamin, whom he taught at seven o'clock, to let him know that they would be starting late today. He also wanted to see his uncle.

'Oh, all right. Thank you. So, I shall see you here then.'

'Yes, I shall be on my way shortly.'

'OK, see you.'

'Bye.'

Shortly after hanging up the phone, Isaac put on his coat and set off. He didn't mind taking the train tonight; as it was Wednesday, he had the next day off from teaching.

He arrived at Sam's house in Sutton. He rang the doorbell, and Alice opened the door. She seemed a bit surprised to see him.

'Oh, Isaac,' she said. 'So sorry; I'm swamped with schoolwork right now.'

'That's fine, no problem,' Isaac assured her. 'I've just come to teach Sam.'

Sam was towards the back, lying on the living room sofa. He looked like he had spent the last half hour or so shifting between being barely awake and lucid dreaming.

'Hey,' greeted Isaac.

Sam, who had his forearm over his brow, squinted whilst looking at Isaac, and said, 'Hey.'

Isaac was starting to wonder whether coming here had been a good idea.

A few seconds later, Sam seemed to realise that Isaac hadn't come to visit but to teach him, so he sat up on the sofa and massaged his face. He yawned.

'Isaac?' spoke a familiar voice from behind.

Isaac turned around immediately, and standing in the dim corridor was his uncle, holding an empty wine glass, who approached and shook his hand.

His uncle looked remarkably like his father: with a small, round face, a small, pointy nose, blue eyes, short, greying hair, and of average height, about an inch or two shorter than Isaac. He was almost like a younger version of his father, so much so that Isaac had to remind himself that the man was only his uncle and that he wasn't obligated to obey him. His countenance was a little friendlier, and he was smiling, perhaps because he was his uncle and, therefore, did not have to demand the same obedience as that towards a father.

'Isaac, it is so good to see you,' he said. He had a soft voice.

'You as well, Uncle David.'

'Wow,' he said, his eyes opened wide as he admired the current image of his nephew, one that he did not have the privilege of seeing very often despite having lived in the same city. 'How have you been?'

'Well, thank you,' said Isaac, nodding and smiling politely.

Sam was sighing, still trying to collect himself. Isaac's uncle did not wear a kippah, but Sam had started wearing one, and his pink kippah had fallen onto the sofa amidst his turning, where it still remained.

'And how is Joseph?' Isaac's uncle asked.

Isaac saw in his eyes how eager he was to learn of his brother's well-being. He did not know what his feelings were regarding his father, but he answered honestly, saying, 'He is very well.'

'Uh-huh,' uttered his uncle. 'Well, please do not let me disturb you. Sam had mentioned that you were coming to study with him.'

'Oh, that's fine,' said Isaac, who reluctantly turned away from him and towards Sleepy Sam, who he roused to be more attentive by patting him on the back. Then, he proceeded with his lesson, his papers with notes in hand. At first, Sam's eyes looked down at the floor, but within minutes, he made eye contact with Isaac, and his questions came soon afterwards.

Throughout this whole lesson, Isaac's uncle sat nearby at the dining table in the adjacent dining room, which connected to the living room. Isaac was too shy to see whether his uncle had been looking in their direction or not. During the first half of the session, there was the sound of silverware clanging against his plate, whereas he was silent during the second half, so he must have been listening and perhaps looking.

Isaac ended the lesson five minutes before he had planned, seeing that drowsiness had overtaken his cousin's eyes, which were now closed.

He got up, and Sam apologised and thanked him for the lesson and for coming. Isaac assured him that there was no need for an apology and that it had been his pleasure. He figured that leaving a bit earlier would give him more time with Benjamin. It was nice to have seen his uncle.

Isaac's uncle saw him out. As Isaac stood outside and his uncle held the door, his uncle said, 'Thank you so much for the lesson over the phone yesterday.'

'You're welcome,' said Isaac. 'I was wondering whether you were able to hear everything.'

'Oh, yes, I definitely was,' said his uncle. 'Yeah, things had always been difficult between me and my brother, unfortunately.'

Isaac did not press for further information, nor did he present it; he was curious to know more about his uncle's relationship with his father, should he choose to disclose it, so he stayed silent and attentive.

'Ever since we were young, I had always been compared to him by my parents,' his uncle confessed. 'Joseph was older, smarter, stronger. This was undeniable in the first years of my life. I suppose having a head start of five years helps. Unfortunately, this included religious matters as well. In Jewish day school, I was struggling. Maybe it's because I had accepted that I was inferior to him. He always had better marks, so I just started to not care. I became less religious shortly after my bar mitzvah, but the thing is, this didn't change anything; this wasn't new; I had always been criticised. So, I thought: I'm going to change this. Maybe I was inferior to my brother, but I was going to try to do better by securing a good profession. So, I went to law school to become a lawyer. My parents didn't approve as I had left my Judaism behind, but I was making good money and finally felt like I had self-respect. I didn't care about Judaism, whatever that was. My parents didn't approve, but they never approved anything I did, so that was no surprise. I think I was seeing and talking to your father less. Then, I fell in love and raised a family. She wasn't Jewish, and so Joseph turned against me. We don't have Mum and Dad in our lives anymore, but Joseph and I don't really talk anymore. I appreciate your coming here. I've found much value in your lessons, so thank you.'

Isaac's uncle nodded, smiling, and the two of them embraced. Isaac then bade him goodbye and went to the station. He had much more clarity and perspective on his uncle's life and relationship with his father but wasn't sure whether it would change nor how his involvement, however intentional or not, could affect that.

CHAPTER XXXII

Following his encounter with his uncle that week, Isaac was now brimming with curiosity and wanted to know his father's perspective. He figured that the worst that could happen would be that his father would refuse to divulge any information. Maybe he could instil peace between the brothers.

So, during Shabbat, he thought about how he would approach his father and figured that Sunday would be a good day to ask when he would be reading *The Sunday Times* on the living room sofa in the late afternoon. This was usually a time when he would be calm and quiet.

When this exact opportunity came, he sat himself next to his father. 'Dad?'

Mr Abrams hummed, engrossed by one of the news articles he was reading.

'Could I talk to you about Uncle David?'

Mr Abrams's eyes looked ahead in confusion and subtle shock before he turned and finally made eye contact with Isaac.

Assuming this meant 'Yes', Isaac asked, 'Do you talk to him often?'

After a few seconds, whose length felt painful to Isaac, Mr Abrams finally said, 'Not particularly.'

'Why don't you?'

'We've always had a difficult relationship. It's complicated,' said Mr Abrams, directing his attention back to the newspaper, though not reading any particular article.

'What did he do to you?' asked Isaac.

'To me?' asked Mr Abrams, sitting up as he looked at Isaac again.

'Yes.'

'Nothing! Not directly, at least. He married a non-Jew, and I had many discussions with him about this. His kids aren't Jewish according to Jewish law, and he's no longer observant, but this is something I don't really want to delve into.'

Isaac was a bit taken aback. His father rarely used the irritated tone he was now using. He didn't want to push him too far, but he wanted to know more about his thoughts and feelings towards this conflict with his brother.

'But Dad! His wife wants to convert now, and his kids! He's even interested in becoming religious too!'

'What?'

'He wants to learn about Judaism! He's even been listening to my lessons over the phone here!'

Mr Abrams's face went pale. Isaac wondered whether he should have exposed this secret and quickly added, 'He hasn't been able to make the lessons.'

Then, Mrs Abrams and Ruth entered the living room, and Mr Abrams resumed staring at the surface of the newspaper, which meant that the conversation was now over.

CHAPTER XXXIII

Isaac's conversation must have affected his father because later that week, the two of them had met at a kosher restaurant. Isaac had found out about this from Sarah, who had been made aware of this by their mother. Isaac's uncle was soon attending Isaac's class in the living room alongside his wife and children. Isaac was truly amazed at the sight of his uncle with his aunt and cousins together at the dining table. He saw that his father was not speaking so much with his uncle whilst he was there, but the amount of progress was undeniable. He was glad to see his uncle was determined to learn about Judaism.

That Shabbat, for whatever reason, Eliezer and Simon had shown up at the synagogue. Isaac, as was usually the case, tried to pay no attention to them. Thomas was coming over for dinner, so Isaac thought to wait for Thomas by his bench as he was still praying. He then saw that Eliezer and Simon were heading in his direction down the aisle, so he got nervous and went around his usual way of leaving the synagogue in order to avoid them, around the front of the section where he sat and up the other aisle. All the members of the synagogue standing around and conversing served as proper obstacles to them ever reaching him. He remembered that once he would be in Israel, whenever that would be, this would no longer be a problem.

He couldn't wait to be in Israel studying again, but he couldn't fantasise about this too much, because if he did, he probably would've constructed a raft after Shabbat to sail across the English Channel and walk from France to Israel all on foot.

He stood by the doors to the sanctuary, and what he saw now was a horrific sight: Eliezer and Simon were now talking to Thomas.

He couldn't look at this any longer; he turned around and went home. Thomas knew where he lived, and his father and Mordechai were still there, should he want to walk home with someone. Why were they talking to Thomas? Had Thomas approached them? Had he spoken to Simon after his surprise visit to the Hanukkah party? When Thomas eventually arrived at his house, Isaac thought about asking him about it, but he preferred to do it when they were alone. Unfortunately, he did not get the opportunity to do so tonight with his family around.

Isaac eventually forgot about this incident. Shabbat was joyful, as always, and it was a pleasure to share the experience with Thomas. On Sunday, Thomas came over for his lesson. Before they began, Thomas, who Isaac had noticed was looking rather serious today, sat at the dining table and said, 'Can I ask you something?'

'I am your teacher,' said Isaac.

'Why don't you talk to your friends?'

Isaac blushed. He knew he could only be talking about his former friends. 'They are not my friends.'

'Why?'

Isaac paused. Was he going to now share with him that he was heartbroken that they had become irreligious? This was too personal to share. So, he refrained from answering.

'Can I be honest with you?' continued Thomas, thus breaking the brief silence. 'I've met all three of them, and I must say that Eliezer, Ari, and Simon are perhaps some of the nicest people I have ever met. In fact, if I hadn't learnt that envying others was forbidden by one of the Ten Commandments, I would've envied you.'

Isaac was suspicious that this hypothetical circumstance was a reality.

'I've become quite friendly with them recently. I respect you, Isaac, and I am really confounded as to why you would go so far as to ignore them when they call your name. I'm even a bit concerned. Is there something I should know about them? You could not treat them this way for no reason.'

Isaac's eyes were downcast. Thomas had resurrected his feelings of sorrow and pain that had long remained dormant.

'I see that it's something private that I should not know about,' remarked Thomas. 'Please excuse me. I apologise if I've been rude. I just couldn't understand. I shall assume that they've hurt you, maybe even unintentionally, but I shall go against your previous recommendation against speaking to them, and I shall continue to spend time with them. I wish the best for all of you. I do like all of you, and I can only hope that this wouldn't complicate anything.'

Isaac nodded, and they started the lesson.

CHAPTER XXXIV

Benjamin rang the doorbell one Wednesday. Isaac opened the door and greeted him. Isaac was so excited to start the next session with him.

Benjamin had grown so much. Isaac had been teaching him for over three months. He now had his own phylacteries and fringes that he wore. He was wearing a kippah everywhere he went, praying at the synagogue three times a day, and he was keeping more and more commandments. He even wore his kippah while working at Gan Eaten. Isaac felt so proud when he saw him wearing it there. Benjamin proceeded to the living room before Isaac when the doorbell rang again.

Isaac wondered who it could be as he headed towards the window. He hadn't invited anyone; no one had indicated they were coming to visit, and everyone in his family had a key.

He looked through the window and saw Ariel outside standing at the top of the front steps. Ariel looked at him and nodded.

Isaac wanted to jump back out of sight; Ariel was the last person he would have expected to turn up without notice.

His heart started pounding more heavily in his chest as he headed towards the front door. If only he had checked through the peephole, he thought. If he had done so, he would have ignored his former friend and pretended like he wasn't there, but because Ariel had seen him, it was no longer possible.

Isaac opened the door. Neither he nor Ariel was smiling.

'Hey,' said Ariel.

'Hi,' said Isaac, not quite sure how to react to this surprise visit.

'May I come in?'

'Sure.'

Isaac stepped aside, letting Ariel in and closing the door after him.

They both stood in the dim entrance. Ariel noticed Benjamin sitting at the dining table in the living room and waved at him.

'Hi,' said Benjamin, waving back, not quite sure what to make of the whole situation.

'I'm Ari,' said Ariel.

'I'm Benjamin, nice to meet you,' replied Benjamin.

'I've seen you at the synagogue,' remarked Ariel.

The two of them didn't move an inch towards each other during their introduction, a phenomenon influenced by Isaac's standing still in the entrance before Ariel. He had asked Isaac to come into the house and nothing else. Isaac, however, was rather upset to see that Benjamin had just met another member of what had been known as The Team.

'How have you been?' asked Ariel, now turning to Isaac.

'Very well, thank you,' said Isaac, trying to keep his facial expressions as neutral as possible.

Ariel was a young man with a stiff upper lip and was mild-mannered, but Isaac knew him, and he saw in his eyes and facial expressions that he was feeling some pain and concern, the same pain and concern that Isaac had felt for his former friends once upon a time.

'I was worried about you. I wanted to come see how you were,' explained Ariel.

'Were you?' said Isaac, though this sounded more like a conclusion than a question.

Ariel continued, 'I've called you several times and left you several text messages.'

'I've been very busy,' was his diplomatic response. Ariel's attempts at communication had lasted for weeks. Isaac hadn't responded to any of them.

'So, we're,' began Ariel, who paused. He stared into Isaac's callous eyes, made what looked like a slight nod, and then looked at Benjamin. 'I see that you're quite busy right now. Please excuse me for showing up without notice. I shall be leaving now.'

Ariel turned around at once and headed out the front door. He stopped briefly to bid Isaac goodbye before descending the steps and heading down the street.

Isaac briefly watched him go before closing the front door. He began his lesson with Benjamin. Benjamin did not ask questions about the incident, nor did Isaac make any comments about it.

CHAPTER XXXV

Isaac found that Sunday was one of his favourite days of the week. On Thursdays, he would spend more time resting after four days of teaching, but Thursdays were always disorganised as he'd try to plan what to do that day as he wouldn't be teaching. He'd miss teaching, even though he wouldn't be doing so to rest. On Fridays, he'd enjoy preparing for Shabbat, but he wasn't particularly productive on that day. On Sundays, he would feel well-rested after Shabbat, full of energy, and ready to tackle the week, and he would finally be able to teach and learn with others again.

After the evening service one Sunday, finding the sky dark as he usually did after service that time of year, he left the synagogue excited to go home. Upon opening the front door of the synagogue, he jumped back. Simon was poised at the top of the steps.

Simon turned around and grinned, exclaiming, 'Isaac!'

Simon embraced him. Isaac couldn't recall having felt so uncomfortable in his life.

When the embrace was finally over (but Isaac's entrapment hadn't fully lifted just yet, as Simon was still holding his arms), Simon said, 'How have you been? I missed you.'

'Good,' said Isaac, wincing.

'I've got news,' he said, now looking and sounding a bit insecure.

Isaac couldn't care less what Simon had to say.

'Eli's getting engaged!'

Isaac's eyes were wide open. 'What?'

'He's getting engaged!' Simon's arms were raised into the air.

Now, Isaac couldn't hold in his curiosity. 'To who?'

'Have you met Margaret?'

Isaac thought of the girl whom he had met, the one who was with Eliezer when he had bumped into him at the supermarket. 'Is she blonde?'

'Yes.'

'With blue eyes, about our height?'

'Yeah, about yours,' clarified Simon, who was but an inch taller than Isaac.

'But she isn't Jewish, is she?'

Simon's jaw hung. He looked completely insecure now. Perhaps this was why he had appeared somewhat unsure when he had brought this up at first. He knew that Isaac wouldn't take it well if Eliezer had been dating a gentile, not to mention engaged to one.

Isaac sighed. He couldn't imagine hearing anything worse. 'Why?'

Simon shrugged. He sulked, seeing that Isaac was clearly disturbed by this.

Isaac commenced several arguments with Eliezer in his mind. How could he date a non-Jew in the first place? Did he not care that his children wouldn't be Jewish? Did he not care that he would be abandoning his heritage? He could feel his face go red, masked in part by the darkness of the night.

'How long have they been engaged?'

'It's not official yet,' said Simon. 'There's still the engagement party. You and I are invited of course!'

Isaac saw that this was also what Simon had wanted to tell him. A part of Isaac then remembered that he wasn't supposed to care about them or talk to them anymore, but now was different. Eliezer was going to make a serious decision that would have long-term consequences, and he needed to know more.

'I've tried calling you several times,' said Simon. 'I knew I'd find you here at this time.'

Simon had been trying to reach him, but Isaac would ignore all of his calls.

After a brief pause, Isaac asked, 'When is the engagement?'

'On Sunday, the First of March,' said Simon.

'That's this coming Sunday,' pointed out Isaac.

Simon nodded.

'Right,' said Isaac, who was engaging in conversation with Simon not because he suddenly cared about him, but because he was now the person who could give him the information he wanted to know, a fact that Simon clearly wasn't aware of.

The two of them descended the steps of the synagogue. Isaac was trying his best to hide his frustration towards Eliezer, as well as not unleashing any of his ire towards Simon. He was no longer friends with Simon, but that didn't give him permission to be cruel to him in any way.

'What time?'

'It starts at one sharp,' said Simon as they now walked on the pavement.

'How do you feel about this?' asked Isaac, turning his head towards him to study his expression.

'I feel great,' said Simon. 'I feel so excited for him; our friend's getting engaged!'

Isaac saw that there was no point in mentioning the harm this would cause due to Margaret's not being Jewish; Simon was already under the spell of unreasonable excitement. He couldn't believe that Simon was being so irrational, so careless out of excitement.

'It's going to be so amazing,' said Simon. 'We're all going to be there! And it shall be at Marge's house.'

Isaac walked in silence. He was now starting to feel overwhelmed with anxiety and shock. What he would have done to find out that this was all a nightmare.

They stopped in front of Isaac's house and Simon finally bade him farewell. Isaac watched as he headed down the pavement and turned out of sight.

He was starting to feel faint. He entered his home, ignoring anyone in his way or saying a simple 'Hi' should anyone greet him as he had to retreat into his bedroom (he couldn't exactly tell who he had encountered along the way). Once there, he had to process everything.

The time had been inching towards the end of February. Spring was just around the corner. The Jewish month of Adar was coming up this week, and with its arrival, a Jew was to increase in happiness. How was he to become happier with the knowledge that a fellow Jew was to become engaged to a gentile?

Eliezer had apparently invited him to the engagement party, but as he no longer was friends with him, he would not go, and how much more so as it was the engagement to a non-Jew.

He then thought about his uncle, who had to go through so much suffering due to having married a gentile, who was now going through the laborious process of converting along with their kids, and not every gentile wife would be willing to do that for her Jewish husband, not to mention their children as well. Was his former friend to become the next David Abrams? And how would his parents react, who he knew were religious? Surely, he knew how upset they would be.

Eliezer had no idea how much damage he was about to do.

PART III

CHAPTER XXXVI

The next day, Isaac received his invitation to Eliezer's engagement by post. After reading through its contents, he tore the letter in half and threw it into the bin as though doing so would blot out the possibility of its ever happening.

But its subject was not something he could resist forever. Later that day, before his session with Thomas would start, Thomas said, 'I'm guessing you've heard of Eli's engagement party?'

As they were neighbours, Isaac imagined the postman had delivered the invitations to them consecutively. Nonetheless, he found it funny how just some months ago, he had been trying to prevent his ever coming in contact with his former friends; it did not bring him half an ounce of pleasure to be discussing Eliezer or his affairs with him now.

'Yes, I have,' answered Isaac.

'Are you going?' asked Thomas; he knew Isaac well enough to know that this was a question.

'No,' said Isaac, his eyes downcast. Then, he raised them towards Thomas again. 'Are you?'

'Of course.'

Isaac was not too surprised. Fortunately, he did not have to evade this topic; Thomas did not get further into it; he must have known that it was against Isaac's intentions.

Isaac now imagined his former friends corrupting his students. Would Benjamin go, too? Had he met Eliezer? Would Thomas go and fancy Margaret's sister if she had one? Would he abandon his decision to convert to Judaism, or worse, convert and marry Margaret's theoretical sister?

After the evening service, upon exiting the synagogue, Isaac jumped again; Simon had been standing outside again that night on the steps. Was this going to be a daily occurrence? Isaac thought.

Simon heard his gasp and turned around.

'Isaac!'

Isaac started considering changing synagogues.

'You've been waiting for me?' he asked.

'Yes!' exclaimed Simon. 'Are you really not going to Eli's engagement party?!'

Who told him this? It had to be Thomas, but he had to verify before accusing anyone. 'Who told you?'

'Thomas,' said Simon.

'No, I'm not going,' said Isaac, his face getting hot. He noticed that Simon was very bothered by this, but this was not something he had wanted to quarrel about.

'Why?!'

'Because I don't support this,' said Isaac, glaring at Simon as he tried to bring him to his senses – someone to his senses out of all of the people in this debacle; clearly, no one had made this attempt to raise their voice against it. 'I'm not going. I'm not going to enable such a thing. I am one hundred per cent not in support of this. This is not to be done, a match not to be made.'

'Who are you to tell someone who to marry?'

This last word made Isaac light-headed; he did not want to think about the next inevitable step.

'It's just wrong,' said Isaac. 'There's just no two ways about it; it's wrong. You're not supposed to marry a non-Jew, nor am I. That's the law. I'm not making this stuff up.'

'OK, but it's his decision,' said Simon.

'And it's my decision not to go.'

'But Isaac, he's our friend.'

Isaac held his tongue; he was not to correct him on this false statement.

'He needs our support. You've *got* to come.'

'No, I haven't,' said Isaac.

'I'm not going to be the one to tell him you're not coming, though I'm sure you shall,' said Simon, whose voice was now getting weaker as he sounded like he was about to sob. His eyes were getting wet. Thankfully, no other congregants were in sight; they had all gone home. Isaac wondered whether Simon was acting this way due to the possibility of his ever marrying a non-Jew and thus Isaac's refusal to attend any wedding or engagement party. 'That's between you and him.'

Isaac kept quiet. Simon had clearly become irrational, which he thought him to be sometimes.

Simon started to cry. Isaac was starting to wonder whether Eliezer would have reacted as strongly. It was his engagement party, after all.

Finally, Isaac, who had no tissue to give, said, 'I think it's time to go home.'

Simon turned and walked down the steps with him. Then, he shook his head and stopped.

'You go ahead. I'm going alone,' said Simon.

'What?' said Isaac.

'I'm going by myself,' said Simon. 'I can't believe you'd do this to Eli.'

Isaac couldn't believe Simon's reaction. He was acting like a kid. He was twenty-one years old, as was Simon, and he was perfectly capable of and entitled to making his own decisions in life. He had decided firmly not to go to the engagement party because he didn't want to send the message to Eliezer that he would support him marrying a gentile. His absence from the engagement party would send the message to the whole community, whose assent by silence was encouraging such a thing.

With Simon's dismissal, he went home. He was starting to feel a little bad, not for refusing to attend Eliezer's engagement party, but for how emotionally wounded he seemed to have made Simon. He was starting to worry he was a bad person. Such were the consequences of maintaining one's values and principles, he supposed.

CHAPTER XXXVII

Isaac's lack of involvement regarding Eliezer's engagement party could no longer continue. He slept for four hours Monday night. Tuesday, whose sunset ushered in the beginning of the month of Adar, was when Isaac was meant to increase in happiness, but he couldn't. The forthcoming engagement 'party' brought him more stress and anxiety than anything else in his life. He had to talk to Eliezer. He had no interest in re-establishing their friendship; he had to confront his former friend and prevent him from making this mistake, which would have consequences that would last forever.

So, on that afternoon during his free time (he would delay his next session should he take too much time), he headed straight to Eliezer's place. There was nothing else he could think about right now.

Clouds meandered like grazing sheep that day in late February. Isaac reached Eliezer's street and ascended the front steps rather confidently, considering that he hadn't exactly planned a speech.

He looked through the bay window and happened to see Eliezer talking to his parents in their living room. Actually, by the looks of it, they were not simply conversing, but quarrelling.

Mr Blume's back was turned against the windows as Eliezer was facing in the direction of the street. Mr and Mrs Blume circled around the room a bit as they spoke, and Isaac saw that Mrs Blume was scowling, her head shaking frantically while communicating to Eliezer. Mr Blume's mouth was opened wide, indicating projections towards his son, though Isaac couldn't hear at all any noise they were making, nor could he make out the words they were saying, except maybe he saw Mr Blume utter the word 'Why', and he saw Eliezer waving his arms whilst hunching his shoulders. He looked quite distressed. Isaac didn't really know what they were saying, but he could imagine what it was about, given the circumstances. He wondered whether they had been arguing like this every day, but he just happened to notice now.

He started feeling a bit bad for Eliezer. He was clearly going through quite a bit of stress. Isaac couldn't imagine having such a heated scene with his parents. Was he going to add more stress to Eliezer's life? He changed his mind about talking to Eliezer; maybe he would talk to him another day or speak to him calmly over the phone.

Then Eliezer noticed Isaac standing outside. His facial expression changed instantly to one filled with joy and relief to the point where Isaac was a bit disturbed by how someone's emotions could change so quickly. Why hadn't I turned around and gone home sooner? thought Isaac, but it was too late; Eliezer had already gone to open the door.

Mr and Mrs Blume looked out the window to see who was there.

Isaac waved and smiled awkwardly at them. They seemed to do the same with less awkwardness.

Eliezer opened the door. 'Isaac!'

'Hey,' said Isaac, turning around to go down the steps. 'Sorry, I see now isn't a good time.'

'No, it's a great time,' insisted Eliezer. 'It's so good to see you! Want to come in?'

'No, it's OK; I shall call you later,' said Isaac, going down the steps and down the street. Isaac was certainly not going to bring up such a discussion amidst his parents' presence.

Eliezer ran after him. 'Wait! No, what is it? What's going on?'

Isaac sighed. 'Nothing. I just needed to talk to you about something, but it's private. We can talk on the phone later.'

'But no one's near now,' said Eliezer, 'We could talk here.'

Isaac looked around. They were the only two people around, though, in Golders Green, that could change within minutes. Isaac sighed again.

'I need to talk to you about the engagement party.'

'I'm so excited!' said Eliezer, grinning, as though that weren't what he and his parents had been quarrelling about just a minute ago. 'Are you coming?'

Isaac sidestepped that question and said, 'I don't think it's a good idea for you to marry this girl. Marge.' Isaac pronounced the name as though it were a word in a foreign language that he had learnt just last week.

'Why?' Eliezer asked much more calmly than Isaac would have expected.

'Because she's not Jewish.'

'So what?'

'So what?! Don't you realise how serious this is? Don't you want your kids to be Jewish? Do you want to just throw away your Jewish heritage, your lineage that reaches back to Mount Sinai?'

'Isaac,' said Eliezer, raising his hand, his face completely unmoved by his words. 'We've been going out for a while now. I want to marry her.'

Isaac was stunned; he could not reason with him. He could think of nothing else to say, no way to persuade him. He had already brought the major points to the table. All he could do was merely repeat the principal arguments or reframe them.

'Are you really going to do this?' asked Isaac.

'I wouldn't have announced my engagement if I wasn't,' said Eliezer.

Isaac only stared at him. Indeed, he barely recognised him. Shortly afterwards, he went back home.

CHAPTER XXXVIII

Simon's shocking appearances were starting to become rather annoying. Not only was this the third night in a row, but he had brought Ariel, too. Isaac jumped at the sight of them standing before the synagogue.

'Would it kill you to come to synagogue?' cried Isaac.

'You're not coming to the engagement party this Sunday?' asked Ariel, looking somewhat insecure to talk to Isaac after their last encounter at his house.

Isaac started descending the steps. He was not going to argue with them in front of the doors to the synagogue.

'Correct, I am not going,' said Isaac.

'Don't you realise how serious this is?' asked Ariel, 'It's Eliezer's engagement.'

Isaac had always thought of Ariel as being the most intelligent of all his former friends. He figured he could reason with him, and perhaps with Simon around, he would follow his example, even if he still wouldn't fully understand.

'Ariel, if I go, that means that I consent to his being engaged to a non-Jew, and I don't.'

'But this would be a big deal if you don't come,' explained Ariel as though Isaac were the one about to sin in this situation. So, Isaac had been wrong about Ariel.

'It would be a big deal if he marries her,' replied Isaac, 'And you know what? He's obviously determined to.'

'But he would be very hurt if you were not to come,' said Ariel.

'He is hurt,' said Simon. 'He already thinks you may not be coming.'

Judging by Simon's emphatic voice, Isaac was starting to wonder whether his and Ariel's visit had been Simon's orchestration.

Isaac had nothing left to say to appease them. He had tried to dissuade Eliezer from going along with the engagement, but that had failed. He was not going to the engagement party. Maybe that would make his former friends upset, but it wouldn't have any practical effect on Isaac; he still wouldn't go out of his way to talk to them anyway. Maybe that would get them to stop with their surprise visits.

'I'm going home,' announced Isaac, 'Have a good night.'

With this assertive statement, Isaac left Simon and Ariel behind outside the synagogue and tried to repress any feelings of guilt for doing so along the way.

CHAPTER XXXIX

Isaac studied with Adam the next day. Afterwards, Isaac had the thought of asking for his opinion regarding not attending Eliezer's engagement party, just to get some confirmation as to how ridiculous it would be to attend such an event. He figured Adam would have an unbiased answer since he wasn't from the neighbourhood and knew nothing of Eliezer.

'Adam, could I ask your opinion about something?'

'Sure,' responded Adam.

'If you were to have a friend who was Jewish and he were to have an engagement party and he was engaged to a non-Jew, would you go?'

Adam sighed. 'That's tough, but I would.'

Isaac tilted his head. 'Would you?'

'Yes,' said Adam. 'I wouldn't date a non-Jew, obviously, but if I were to skip my friend's engagement party, I think that would make him very sad.'

'But wouldn't you think that that would be enabling his marrying the non-Jew?'

'Well, practically speaking, what are the odds of him changing his mind just because one friend didn't show up?'

Isaac thought about it.

Amidst Isaac's silence, Adam continued, 'I'm not condoning his decision, nor am I saying that what I would do is the right thing or the wrong thing, but that's just what I would do, if my friend were to get engaged.'

Isaac nodded. Then, he couldn't help himself from admitting the truth. 'My friend is getting engaged to a non-Jew. The engagement party is this Sunday, and up until now, I was surely not going.'

Adam raised his eyebrows. 'Oh. Wow. Well, you wouldn't at least go for your friend?'

Isaac shook his head. 'I'm torn. I really don't know what to do.'

'Have you spoken to him about this?'

'He knows what my stance is on this,' said Isaac.

'Well, it's up to you,' said Adam, 'but if you don't go – I'm not sure how close you are with him – I would imagine that he'd be very hurt.'

Isaac pondered on this last word. If only Eliezer had known how much hurt he had caused him.

CHAPTER XL

That Sunday morning, just a few hours before the engagement party was to start, Isaac had to call Simon in order to get the address of Margaret's house after he had torn up the invitation card. As he walked up Margaret's street, which wasn't too far from where Eliezer lived, he had a very bad feeling about attending the engagement party, and he hadn't had an awful feeling like this in a very long time. Last time he checked, he was no longer friends with Eliezer, but the absence from someone's engagement party, of one who he had known for a very long time – even if they were a former associate – would have left him with so much guilt he would've been unable to live with himself. Even if he were never to speak to Eliezer again. He saw this as the beginning of the official end of their relationship. Yes, Margaret would be with him and keep him preoccupied, thus his choosing to disassociate from him would no longer be so obvious, assuming he would no longer request for more of his time.

He ascended the front steps, and Mrs Phillips opened the door. The house was filled with popular, cheerful music that could not influence Isaac's irritated mood in any way, but he smiled only for Eliezer.

'Oh, welcome!' said Mrs Phillips, throwing her arms in the air. 'And who might this be?'

'Oh, that's my friend, Isaac!' said Eliezer, who popped out of the living room with Margaret, thus saving Isaac from uttering a similar statement, which would've been a lie.

Margaret approached Isaac and gave him a hug.

Suddenly, Isaac felt faint. He was so uncomfortable. His face went red. Had Margaret's mother not been there, he probably would have made a calamity out of this.

He took a step back, and Margaret, whose face was beaming and grinning, now seemed a bit surprised by the gesture.

'Welcome,' said Eliezer as if it were his home.

Isaac wanted to mention that he was not to hug women, but by the time his shock and anxiety had dissipated, Mrs Phillips and Margaret had re-entered the living room, and Eliezer, who had a glass of champagne in his hand, told Isaac, 'Come on in!'

Isaac followed him into the living room. There were about two dozen other young adults, mostly friends of Eliezer and Margaret, as well as some relatives of theirs. Mr and Mrs Blume were sitting on the sofa by the windows quietly as though they were attending a funeral instead. Mr Blume wasn't wearing his kippah. Thomas, Ariel, and Simon were there chatting near the wall.

Isaac was really sad as he kept reminding himself that the only reason why he was here was because Eliezer was to marry a non-Jew. He drifted throughout the room until he wound up by Thomas, Ariel, and Simon, though this latter group was much quieter than the other young adults. Eventually, Thomas got bored and decided to venture out and socialise with the other young adults. Isaac didn't utter a word, only listening to the occasional remark made by Simon or Ariel.

Eventually, Margaret and her parents started serving food, and some people started taking seats. Isaac, Simon, and Ariel sat by the dining table.

Margaret appeared with some food trays. 'Hey. I know you guys only eat kosher food, so we've got these for you.'

She handed them the trays, and there was a fourth one in her hand, which she would give to Thomas.

'Wow, thank you so much,' said Simon.

'Thank you,' said Ariel and Isaac.

Isaac couldn't help but notice that Eliezer ate what everyone else did. Margaret would then distribute two more of these trays to Mr and Mrs Blume.

As Isaac, Simon, and Ariel began consuming their meals (Thomas had been handed his, but he was too distracted by his conversation with others to start), Ariel, who was sitting to Isaac's right by their end of the extended dining table, said to Isaac, 'You know, when I had gone to your place before, I had meant to tell you about the engagement.'

Isaac looked at Ariel after he had said this. Ariel's eyebrows were raised.

Isaac didn't know what Ariel was trying to insinuate, but he wondered whether he could have prevented this if he had found out about the engagement sooner when Ariel wanted to tell him. Before Eliezer would have announced the engagement party. Before he would have fallen more in love with Margaret. This idea of a missed opportunity was starting to depress him.

Margaret was looking quite stunning. Her face glowed with joy. She had her blonde hair tied back, and she wore a flowing white dress. She went here and there around the room, entertaining the guests and making sure that they were comfortable. Eliezer was talking to her siblings and cousins. He was establishing rapport with his future in-laws.

Isaac stared at Eliezer as he spoke with Margaret's friends, who joined the group.

'I just want to make a toast,' announced Mr Phillips, standing in the middle of the room, raising his glass of champagne, 'to my beloved daughter Margaret and her soon-to-be-husband, Eliezer, for a long-standing, happy, wonderful marriage! Cheers!'

'Cheers!' said everyone except Isaac and Eliezer's parents, the latter of whom raised their glasses of sparkling water whilst omitting the word.

Then came the sudden sound of a woman singing in a high-pitched tone. At first, Isaac thought it was from the music that they had selected to play on speakers, but there was no instrumentation; he turned around and, to his shock, he saw that it was Margaret with a microphone singing right behind him.

Isaac jumped. He froze. He was not allowed to listen to a woman sing! He couldn't just tell her to stop, not in this context, so he instinctively got up and walked to the adjacent kitchen where there were other guests conversing, which meant it wouldn't look too socially inappropriate for him to stay there. It wouldn't be too obvious that he was avoiding her singing.

He could still hear the singing clearly.

He looked around. There were five other people in the kitchen, none of whom he knew. He covered his ears and started humming to himself loudly to block out the sound of her singing. The five other people in the kitchen started looking at him as if he were insane.

'Yeah, I can't stand my sister's singing, either,' said one of them, though Isaac saw that he had meant this sarcastically; he looked quite offended that one of the guests had left the room where his sister had been singing during her engagement party.

Ariel came to the kitchen, looking somewhat concerned.

'Isaac, are you all right?'

'No,' said Isaac, whispering and turning his head to face the adjacent wall so as not to cause any more offence, as he was now not facing in the direction of Margaret's brother whilst talking, 'I'm not allowed to hear a woman sing.'

'I'm not sure if we could just tell her to stop,' said Ariel. 'It's OK.'

Isaac looked at Ariel, seeing the concern that he seemed to have for him. It was then that he felt nostalgic for the times he had spent with his friends, and now it all seemed to be falling into ruin. Ariel had always been a caring person, showing concern for Isaac's welfare.

What was so wrong about them? Sure, Eliezer was now to marry a non-Jew, but did it warrant casting him out of his life? And what had Simon and Ariel done that had warranted this treatment?

He didn't have time to ponder this as Margaret rushed into the kitchen. Isaac's eyes opened wide in shock as he saw that she was running up to him, looking worried.

'Isaac, hey,' she said, still looking concerned.

'Hi,' he said. Had she read his thoughts?

'I meant to ask you, have I by any chance offended you by hugging you before? If so, I'm so sorry.'

'Well, yes, but you didn't know,' said Isaac.

'I'm so sorry,' she said. 'Eliezer told me you were a hugger! If I had known it would've offended you, I wouldn't have done it.'

Isaac wouldn't have denied himself the title of 'hugger' when it was permissible, nor was he particularly known for hugging, either.

'What do you mean? He told you I'm a hugger?' asked Isaac.

'Well, yeah. He told me to,' she said, now looking regretful.

'He told you to hug me?'

'Yeah,' she said under her breath. And then she said, as if to apologise for Eliezer's sake, 'I'm so sorry!'

Isaac couldn't restrain himself any longer. What had he just been doing, meditating on the reasons why he had dissociated himself from his friends? Such reasons were beyond obvious! Here he was, reluctantly attending Eliezer's engagement party, and he had instructed her to embrace him when he knew that he was not allowed to do such a thing!

He was consumed in ire. He couldn't stay here any longer, lest he start a calamity or do something else destructive in congruence with his frustration. He went out of the kitchen and through the living room. He could not bear to look at Eliezer.

He had known that coming here was a bad idea. Little had he known that it would lead to this. He could not have imagined it. He hadn't realised that Eliezer would have such malicious intentions! He would not speak, let alone look at him anymore!

He opened the front door and let himself out. Maybe someone there, like Margaret's brother, would have taken issue with that, but he was in fact doing them a favour; it was the mildest reaction he could have thought of after hearing what Margaret had to say. Should Eliezer try to stop him now, he would not listen.

As Isaac headed down the street, Eliezer did not stop him or come out of the house and call his name.

It was then he remembered the discomfort he felt from Margaret's singing. He had told her to sing, too! What was next, that the food wasn't kosher? What had Eliezer ordered for them, food that was halal or, worse, vegan?

It had been a mistake to come to the engagement party. Should Eliezer decide to go through with the wedding, Isaac would not make the mistake of attending.

CHAPTER XLI

Several days after the engagement party was Purim. During the days between these aforementioned events, Isaac had been able to cope after the engagement party by pretending as though it had never existed. He threw a Purim party, which he organised with his family. His family, Thomas, Benjamin, Adam, and Pinchas came. He had invited his cousins, aunt, and uncle, from Manchester, but they had already made plans for Purim, which saddened Isaac. He had also invited Simon and Ariel; there could be no harm in extending to them the opportunity to reengage with Judaism, but to his surprise, they had already made plans, too.

So, as Isaac sat down in his lobster costume (Benjamin was dressed as one of Father Christmas's elves, Adam as a chef, Pinchas as Darth Vader, and Thomas as himself because he thought that Isaac's direction to dress up 'like it's Halloween' couldn't have possibly been a thing), he had – perhaps with the influence of the wine – a sudden insight. Perhaps there was a way to end the engagement of Eliezer and Margaret. Surely, they were too determined to marry – God-forbid – at this point, but an earnest recommendation to her parents against the marriage by someone who knew the fiancé would be a good way to accomplish this. Yes, he thought, he would do this on

Sunday during his free time. This helped him celebrate the rest of Purim with more joy and enthusiasm.

So, that Sunday, he headed to Mr and Mrs Phillips's house, the last place he could've imagined going to a week ago. He didn't have their phone number, nor wanted it, so he had to show up unannounced, but he could still postpone if Margaret's parents were too busy or weren't there. After he rang the doorbell and stood waiting before the front door, he considered that should one of their children be home, he'd have to request for them to speak privately with him in some room.

Mrs Phillips opened the door, clutching her white poncho and looking quite surprised but also joyful to see Isaac again.

'Oh, hello! I'm so sorry. What is your name again?'

'Isaac.'

'Oh, right, please, do come in.'

'Thank you,' said Isaac politely, trying to deny any remembrance of the trauma he had experienced in this very house. 'Are any of your children here, if I may ask?'

'Oh, no. It's just me and my husband. Please, come in,' she said, entering the living room, where she beckoned him over.

He followed and obeyed her hand gestures to sit on the sofa opposite the doorway to the entrance.

'Do you take tea or coffee?' asked Mrs Phillips.

'Oh, no, I'm fine. Thank you so much,' said Isaac. 'I actually just wanted to speak to you and Mr Phillips, if I may.'

'Oh, of course,' she said. She rose from the sofa opposite Isaac and headed into the kitchen, from where she withdrew Mr Phillips.

The living room was actually quite beautifully designed, Isaac noticed. Such was a place easier to enjoy and much more peaceful when Eliezer wasn't around.

Mr and Mrs Phillips sat down on the sofas opposite Isaac.

'So, what would you like to discuss?' asked Mrs Phillips, smiling though Mr Phillips looked slightly more sceptical.

Isaac studied Mrs Phillips's smile, and he felt bad. She must have expected some encouraging news regarding the expected wedding. She must have been so happy and excited. That they were being so welcoming and hospitable to him didn't help, but only made him feel more guilty for what he planned to do.

'I'd like to discuss something regarding Eliezer and Margaret's engagement,' he said, watching Mrs Phillips's head lean forward in anticipation. 'I would like to voice my recommendation against the marriage between Eliezer and your daughter.'

Mrs Phillips gasped, covering her mouth with her hands. Mr Phillips winced in confusion.

'What?' said Mr Phillips.

Mrs Phillips was stunned but recovered and asked, 'Why?'

'You should know something about Eliezer,' began Isaac. 'I have known him for a very long time, since secondary school, and there are many character traits that I am very well aware of that one may not notice immediately, and the truth is that Eliezer can be quite temperamental – and awkward. He's struggled socially throughout his entire life – he threw a pie at my face on my birthday once in school. He's spent a lot of time bullying me and others throughout our childhood, and many people have and still look down on him.' Isaac couldn't believe how easily he could have come up with these lies.

'It's funny how such a young man would still attract your friendship after such apparent misbehaviour,' said Mr Phillips sternly. Then, he seemed to recollect some ease and light-heartedness. 'Nonetheless, it's amazing how someone who could be so unpopular could attract so many guests.'

Isaac saw that Mr Phillips didn't believe him. He was starting to wonder whether he could read minds, too, and had passed this trait onto his daughter.

So, he turned to Mrs Phillips in one last desperate attempt, also seeing that Mr Phillips was now looking at the carpeted floor. He figured he might as well be honest, but before he could continue his discourse, Mrs Phillips said, 'We have known Eliezer for months, and we have always found him to be an exceptional young man.'

'During the engagement party, there was a point where Marge hugged me,' he confessed. 'I am not allowed to hug a woman who is not a close relative of mine. Eliezer knew this, yet he had told her to hug me. Also, he had told her to sing, and I am not allowed to hear her sing!'

Mrs Phillips shook her head. 'No, it was Marge's idea to sing. She loves to sing, and if she had known that you would have been offended, she wouldn't have done it. Eliezer had nothing to do with that.'

Mr Phillips now looked nauseated by Isaac's presence.

Isaac now felt silly after having come here. So, it hadn't been Eliezer who had told her to sing, he thought, but he had still told her to hug him.

'Isaac,' said Mrs Phillips, 'we really appreciate your warning, but we can decipher between good and bad characters, and we are both confident in Marge's decision that Eliezer is the right man for her, and we are very happy and excited for our daughter.'

At least I tried, thought Isaac. He sighed and got up. 'OK, well, if you are confident in your decision, then so be it. Please excuse me if I have wasted your time.'

'No, not at all!' insisted Mrs Phillips.

Mr Phillips remained silent, still staring at the carpet.

Mrs Phillips got up to follow Isaac to the entrance.

'Have a good day,' murmured Mr Phillips.

'You, too,' said Isaac as he entered the entrance.

Mrs Phillips opened the front door.

Isaac couldn't help feeling so ridiculous, and this feeling would linger for a long time, long after Mrs Phillips had smiled as she had bidden him goodbye before he had descended the front steps after that failed mission.

CHAPTER XLII

Isaac had no choice but to accept the engagement. He had tried every possible way to end it. He had tried to dissuade Eliezer from going along with it, and he had tried to discourage Mr and Mrs Phillips from letting their daughter marry him.

However, Isaac still held resentment against Eliezer for having schemed against him in the engagement party by having orchestrated his embrace with Margaret. These feelings preoccupied him so much that after two days of fixating on this, which involved losing hours of sleep and being distracted from his teaching and studies, he resolved to confront Eliezer about this. It was obviously the only way to get him back to carrying on normally.

On Tuesday afternoon, two days after his visit to the home of the Phillips family, he phoned Eliezer and asked whether he could speak to him face-to-face. Eliezer replied that he'd be home in a couple of hours.

At the designated time, Isaac headed to Eliezer's place and knocked on the front door. He waited outside, and the fresh breeze of the middle of March swept past him, that promising sense and sign of spring to come, but he was feeling intimidated and anxious; such was not the way he preferred to be greeted by these seasonal introductory delights.

Eliezer opened the door with a neutral expression on his face. He must have known that anything was possible.

'Can I speak to you privately?' requested Isaac.

'Mind if we talk outside?' suggested Eliezer.

'Not at all,' said Isaac.

They descended the steps and stood on the pavement. There were no pedestrians around at the time.

'I want you to know that I am deeply hurt and offended by what you had done to me at the engagement party,' said Isaac, and seeing Eliezer's expression swiftly change to one of defence, he quickly specified: 'I know that you had told Margaret to hug me upon greeting me when you know that I would've been uncomfortable with that because it's not allowed.'

Eliezer crossed his arms and nodded as he scowled. 'Yeah.'

Isaac was a bit caught off guard; he hadn't expected Eliezer to admit to it so quickly. 'I'm very upset about that –'

'I did that to teach you a lesson,' interrupted Eliezer.

'Teach me a lesson?' asked Isaac.

'Yeah,' said Eliezer. 'I wanted you to know and realise that we're not all perfect and some of us may make mistakes and, because you made that mistake, it doesn't mean that everyone should start judging you.'

'What do you mean?' exclaimed Isaac. 'That wasn't a mistake; that was planned out by you!'

'Yeah,' said Eliezer, as if he had forgotten.

'How could you do such a thing?' yelled Isaac, frustrated that he still hadn't received an apology or any amount of understanding.

'You want to know why?' said Eliezer. 'Here's why. Ever since you came back from yeshiva, you've changed. You've become a completely different person. You've become critical and intolerant of everything anyone does wrong – in your eyes.

You've also become arrogant. You really act like you know and do better than everyone else. I don't know who you are anymore, Isaac! I don't know what happened to you! I know you don't want me to marry Marge, but I'm going to do so anyway because that's what I want to do! Gosh, when was the last time I ever told you how to live your life? What are you even doing now, anyway?'

Isaac hesitated. Amidst Eliezer's reddened face, was he seriously awaiting an answer to that question?

'I'm not an idiot, Isaac,' Eliezer continued, 'I know that you're ignoring me. I don't know if it's something I've done; maybe it's because I'm not as religious as I used to be, but you look down on me. I see it. You've got contempt for me. You don't talk to Simon or Ari, either. Well, you know what, Isaac? I see what you're doing. I notice the silent treatment you've been giving me. I love you, Isaac; we've been best friends for so many years, and what you're doing hurts me. It hurts so bad, you've got no idea, but I can't let this go on forever. You've got to decide whether we're still going to be friends or not.'

There were now one or two passers-by around, and Isaac froze amidst this public humiliation. He saw the redness in Eliezer's moist eyes. His heart felt sore, and he felt his eyes getting moist too. Was he going to cry out here in public? he thought fearfully.

'Think about it. You decide,' said Eliezer, now turning away, and saying, 'I'm glad you've grown. I'm so happy you enjoyed your time in yeshiva in Israel. I'm sorry for what I did at the party. It was wrong. Please forgive me.'

Isaac was still frozen. This paralysis was the reason for which he did not respond to Eliezer, not because he hadn't accepted his apology.

With whatever way Eliezer interpreted his omission, he continued his way back to his house, not once looking back, and shut the front door behind him.

Isaac turned around and walked home as if nothing had just happened, still feeling sad and embarrassed. He had never realised just how much hurt and pain he had caused Eliezer, not to mention Simon and Ariel. He had only been focusing on the pain they had inflicted upon him. Maybe they felt more pain, and this was something that resulted from his deliberately ignoring them. He started to feel sick upon approaching the façade of his home.

When he arrived, he opened the door and saw that he had received a letter by post. It was from Eliezer.

He opened it and saw that it contained an invitation card for the wedding of Eliezer Blume and Margaret Phillips, which was to take place at a stately home in Central London on Sunday, the Fifth of April.

CHAPTER XLIII

Isaac's immediate reaction to reading the invitation letter was to come up with excuses for not going. Perhaps it was during the times of mourning or during festivals when weddings couldn't be held. That would by default prevent him from attending. He looked at the Jewish calendar in the kitchen and saw that the Fifth of April was three days before the beginning of Passover, so that excuse couldn't be made.

He considered visiting his cousin Daniel in Manchester, but was this the proper move after their relationship had been so strained? He also didn't want to cancel any of his teaching and learning lessons by travelling up north.

Several days passed, and he still couldn't focus as easily during his teaching and studying sessions. He couldn't believe that the marriage between Eliezer and Margaret was to become a reality.

That Shabbat, Thomas had meals with Rabbi Levy and his family. Benjamin was attempting to do Shabbat at his place.

As it was just Isaac and his family this Shabbat, Isaac had more time to reflect on things in solitude.

He came to realise that a lot of the unease he had felt that week was due to the guilt he felt over the way he had been treating his friends.

He loved his friends Eliezer, Simon, and Ariel. What had been so wrong that they had done to merit Isaac's coldness, disdain, and lack of communication? The only malicious act that he could have come up with was what Eliezer had told Margaret to do at the engagement party, but he had already forgiven Eliezer for that. He was willing to put that behind him.

Isaac now pondered on all these thoughts after he had retired into his dark bedroom that Shabbat night as he sat on his bed.

Whatever he could have been upset about regarding his friends' lifestyles could not compare to their spectacular character traits. Thomas was right. The truth was that all three of them had always been loyal to him. He thought about what Thomas had told him in the living room regarding them, that these friends were enviable. He hadn't seen the value then. Simon was always cheerful and a pleasure to be around, Ariel was always intelligent and upright, and Eliezer was always considerate and affectionate. How much damage Isaac had done to them. How could they ever forgive him for this?

He had to go to the wedding. He had spent the last countless months trying to get his friends to change their ways, to stop the wedding from ever happening, but all the time and effort spent on these endeavours had been in vain. He wasn't going to change anyone. He couldn't change anyone. The question was whether he was going to keep them as friends or not.

Isaac wanted nothing other than to be with his friends, to reclaim the former status of their friendships, as though he could have made whatever had happened these past many months no longer exist, but tears started to form in his eyes because he knew that this was not possible. So much wasted time! So much time that could have been spent on love, growth, or shared experiences was gone and wasted in resentment, contempt, and arrogance. He could not live with himself, but sleep came in time.

The next morning, Isaac knew that he couldn't see his friends just yet during Shabbat. After the morning services, he approached Rabbi Gold and asked him how Simon was doing, and he in turn said that he was doing well. He spent much time later thinking about his friends, excited to see them again – any of them. However, it would be much more challenging as his timetable was a lot more packed.

That Sunday, he called Eliezer to make him aware that he intended to go to his house. He wanted to tell him that he had forgiven him and had no ill feelings towards him whatsoever. He left a voicemail, and as he only had so much free time before his next session, he decided to go to his house anyway and talk to him.

He rang the doorbell to his house. After opening the door, Mrs Blume said that he was not there. He had gone to the United States to visit relatives and go sightseeing with Margaret. He would be gone for ten days and return on the First of April.

Later that week, still plagued by a lack of concentration during the sessions, Isaac rang Simon and Ariel and asked whether they wanted to come for Shabbat, but they both couldn't make it as they had already made plans. When Isaac asked them what they would be doing out of innocent curiosity, they gave vague responses.

That Shabbat, Thomas and Benjamin were both having the Shabbat meals at Rabbi Levy's house. Isaac's relatives in South London were now mostly keeping Shabbat in their home; they, except for Mr Abrams, couldn't keep Shabbat fully as they hadn't yet converted, and Shabbat could only be kept by Jews.

This meant that Isaac spent this Shabbat with a lot of alone time as well. He was feeling a bit sad, a bit isolated this Shabbat. He would have liked to be with Thomas and Benjamin at Rabbi

Levy's house, but of course, he wouldn't have thought to invite him as his family already kept Shabbat. He then started to wonder why Simon and Ariel hadn't accepted his invitation. Maybe they just didn't want to see him? Was it too late to re-establish their friendship? It had been a while since either of the two had initiated contact with him, even if it had been partially – perhaps mostly – his fault. He cringed. Had he lost his friends?

He hated to admit to himself how bitterly awful he felt throughout this Shabbat, as Shabbat was supposed to be a time of joy and pleasure. The truth was, this uncertainty over his friends' stances regarding the state of their friendships had been the same painful uncertainty he had brought all three of them over the past several months.

He concluded that he would see Simon and Ariel again at the wedding, which as of Saturday night, was now eight days away.

Eliezer arrived back in London on Wednesday. Isaac had no idea what time he would arrive exactly, so he decided to give it a day and have his conversation with Eliezer the day after his arrival, which would be easier for him as he didn't teach on Thursdays.

Around noon on Thursday, Isaac phoned Eliezer and asked him whether he could go over to his house. Eliezer sounded rather ill. He asked whether he could come over to Isaac's place, which made him excited to know that he would be able to see a member of The Team, and it would be more convenient for him. He accepted. This would give them privacy as no one else was in the house.

Moments later, Eliezer rang the doorbell. Isaac opened it, saw him, and embraced him. This lasted for several seconds, and it felt like he hadn't seen Eliezer in such a long time. Isaac then started to cry.

'I'm sorry,' Isaac said in Eliezer's jacket.

'For what?' Eliezer replied, sounding as though he were about to cry too.

'For the silence.'

'It's OK,' said Eliezer, shaking his head, then looking at Isaac.

'I want you to know I forgive you for what happened at the party,' said Isaac, looking up at Eliezer. 'Please come in.'

Eliezer walked in and Isaac closed the front door.

The house was filled with silence. The wooden floor creaked with Eliezer's footsteps, and Eliezer gazed around the living room as if he had never been there before. He sighed, and the sigh sounded as though it contained cathartic relief. Isaac saw all this behind eyes wet in tears, his vision now blurry.

Eliezer sat down at the dining table, looking down as he covered his eyes with his hand. He sat at the same table where Isaac's students and study partners would sit. Isaac gazed at the image of his friend who was about to be married.

Eliezer started shaking his head.

Isaac assumed that Eliezer was feeling what he was more intensely and for the same reason.

'That trip,' said Eliezer, still shaking his head whilst covering his eyes.

'Oh yeah, how was it in the States?' asked Isaac, his voice trembling.

'Horrible,' Eliezer said under his breath.

'Why?' asked Isaac, his voice cracking. He sniffed.

Eliezer paused. 'My family. You should've seen them.'

Isaac stopped asking questions and let his friend speak.

'I went there thinking that I would introduce the girl I'm in love with, my fiancée, to my family, that they would embrace her, that we would go out and visit different tourist destinations, and see landscapes. I had planned to stay at my aunt's for a week, but I left after two days. You should've seen them, Isaac.'

Eliezer sighed and then looked up at Isaac. 'My family there is really religious. They treated us like outcasts. You should've seen it. It wasn't so obvious, but you could just feel it. My aunt, my cousins, they just didn't talk to me the same way as before, *look* at me the same way.'

Eliezer then started to sob. Isaac took the tissue box from the bookshelf and placed it on the dining table beside him. He grabbed a couple, dried his eyes, and blew his nose. He sniffed.

'I could never forget it. They hardly talked to Marge. I thought, why am I here? So we rented a room in a hotel and spent the rest of the time visiting tourist attractions and we saw some of the mountains up north in New York. Not even a call from them.

'You don't understand, Isaac. I was well aware of what I was getting into. I knew it from the start, but had I ever imagined that it would lead to this? No. I did not expect this. My parents are angry with me. I'm going through with this marriage, and I don't even have my parents' blessing. Now my family in the States don't want anything to do with me on top of that?

'This is just so difficult, Isaac! It's so hard! Have you ever been in love? Do you realise how difficult this is for me? Have you ever loved someone so much, Isaac?'

Isaac was taken aback by Eliezer's desperate expression. He couldn't say that he had ever been in love, but he was unsure if now was the right time to speak.

'What should I do?' Eliezer asked, now looking up again. 'What do I do?'

Isaac swallowed. He knew his only suggestion would not be accepted.

Eliezer sighed and shut his eyes. It looked like he was finally calming down.

That was what Eliezer needed, Isaac noticed. Someone to talk to. He just wanted – needed – care and love. This was what he had been denying him for so long. He sat on the chair beside him and patted him on the back.

Eliezer sighed and said, 'Thank you for listening.'

Isaac nodded. He didn't know what to say. The wedding was in three days. There was no sign of its cancellation. All he could do was listen, so that was what he did. That next day, however, he would meet with Pinchas. He had planned to spend time with him and maybe learn a little.

CHAPTER XLIV

Isaac met with Pinchas the next day in the living room. They chatted for a bit, then learnt together and chatted some more, and it was during this time when Isaac wanted to speak to Pinchas about a personal subject he had wanted to bring up with him.

'Pinchas, do you think that I'm critical?' asked Isaac.

'No, why?'

'No reason,' said Isaac, looking down at the dining table. 'I've got a question: if someone were too critical, how could one become less critical?'

'You've just got to focus on the positive aspects of people,' said Pinchas.

Isaac thought about the positive aspects of people.

'You just need to actively look for positive things you love about people,' continued Pinchas. 'Why, has someone called you critical?'

Isaac ignored the question. He was not going to summarise all the things that had happened in the last eight or so months regarding his friends.

'To look for the positive things in people,' said Isaac slowly, nodding, 'actively.'

'Yeah,' said Pinchas. 'Let's practise. Can you tell me one positive thing about me?'

One positive thing about Pinchas? Of course, he could tell him one positive thing about him; he had made him his study partner. Why would he ask him such an obvious question? Surely, there had been at least one good thing about him that would have informed him to make that decision, but come to think of it, he could be a bit delayed in his responses, which secretly upset Isaac and even worried him at times, as he would wonder whether he had heard what he had just said. He hadn't been like that when they were younger. Right, one positive thing about Pinchas.

'I think you've got good principles,' said Isaac, nodding confidently.

'Do you? Could you be more specific?'

Isaac wondered whether this was for the purpose of this exercise or for his ego. Nonetheless, it did take him some time to answer. 'You're very serious about Torah. You've been observant since we were young, and I respect that.'

'Thank you,' said Pinchas, grinning. 'You see? You've got it.'

Isaac thought about how he could use this advice with his friends. What was one positive thing about Eliezer? He was loyal. What was one positive thing about Simon? He cared about Isaac. And Ariel? He was always true to his word; he was trustworthy.

Isaac appreciated Pinchas's teaching. He hoped that this knowledge would help him in his friendships. Although he loved his friends, he could still improve his relationships, and this would be a helpful tool he could use with them. It would surely help at the wedding, which was now two days away.

CHAPTER XLV

Isaac tried to put to use Pinchas's advice throughout the rest of the week, particularly in preparation for the wedding, so that he could at least tolerate it with inner peace. He used it on Shabbat with Mordechai, his mother, father, sisters, and Thomas, who was their guest for Shabbat dinner, much as he already loved them.

He was too distracted to study Sunday morning for more than half an hour of proper concentration. He had cancelled his sessions for the rest of the day due to the wedding. He felt absolutely nervous, almost as if he were feeling the nervousness for Eliezer.

The time to depart had come. He headed to the train station. It was a fifteen-minute ride in the underground to Central London. It was an odd feeling to help his mother remove chametz from the house and then attend his friend's wedding.

As he walked down the pavement outside, it was like there was an invisible barrier he had to push through with his footsteps. Suddenly, he debated whether he should go. His uncertainties remained throughout the rest of the walk.

On his journey the weather shifted rapidly – first the sky featured patches of blue, then golden sunlight, now it was overcast.

He had a black suit on and a white dress shirt with black trousers. He had chosen to wear a blue tie. He didn't think about the future, what could come out of this, but only of the present. It would drive him mad to dwell on that which was beyond his control. Should he turn around and go home? It was too late now; he had arrived just outside the stately home where the wedding would take place. Simon and Ariel were approaching opposite him on the pavement, smiling at him. How happy he was to see them. It was like a reunion.

He embraced them, and they entered the home.

They entered the reception room where the only people Isaac recognised were Simon, Ariel, and Thomas, who came a few minutes later. They stayed close together as they conversed.

Isaac sought to pay as close attention as possible to his conversations with them. It was a pleasure to be with Simon and Ariel again. He contained his excitement so as not to overwhelm them. He forgot for a while that he was attending a wedding. There were refreshments served, but the food wasn't kosher. It didn't come as a huge surprise to Isaac. The only people who kept kosher here were him, Mr and Mrs Blume, and Thomas. Also, Thomas hadn't converted yet, so he could have still eaten the non-kosher food if he wanted to, but he chose not to. There were speakers around that played 'Country House' by Blur. A photographer was taking pictures of the guests from every corner of the room. Isaac studied the faces around. He wondered how they knew Eliezer and Margaret.

Mr and Mrs Phillips eventually came, as well as Mr and Mrs Blume, and, as there were easily over a hundred attendees, Isaac and his friends hadn't got a chance to speak to them when it was time to proceed to the drawing room opposite to the reception room out in the entrance. Isaac wanted the event to be over with.

There, Isaac was able to sit in the same row as Thomas, who sat to his left, and Simon and Ariel, who sat to his right. There were rows of seats divided by a wide aisle. There was a black piano and a microphone stand at the front. Isaac found it a bit odd that there was mixed seating amongst the genders. He looked around. He assumed that many of the guests here weren't Jewish. After having spent so much time in yeshiva or in other Jewish environments, it was an odd feeling to be at this event.

All the attendees conversed before the next part of the wedding was to begin. The sky darkened outside. As none of the lights were on in the room, the whole room darkened with it.

'Looks like it's about to rain,' observed Simon.

'I hope it doesn't; the wedding's supposed to take place outside,' said Ariel.

'Really?' said Isaac.

'Yeah,' said Ariel.

Isaac fantasised that it would rain and the wedding would be cancelled.

'I guess they shall move it inside if it starts to rain,' said Thomas.

Simon shrugged. 'I don't know.'

Mr Phillips appeared alongside Mrs Phillips, Mr and Mrs Blume, Margaret, and Eliezer, who all sat in the front row.

Mr Phillips got up. He stood by the microphone and gave a speech on how proud he was of his daughter and how much he admired Eliezer. Mrs Phillips spoke after, followed by Mr Blume, whose speech was short and polite.

Then, a group of hired musicians performed a few pieces of music, some songs and some instrumentals. Isaac noticed that all the singers were male. He wondered whether this decision had anything to do with making Mr and Mrs Phillips aware that he couldn't listen to Margaret sing or maybe because Eliezer had helped plan it that way since he knew that Isaac and all the other Jewish men attending couldn't hear women sing. They could've served some kosher options at the reception. After the performance, which had made Simon fall asleep, they were all welcome to take part in some more non-kosher refreshments.

The sky got a bit brighter outside. It looked like Isaac's fantasy, however far-fetched, would not come true. But to his surprise, Ariel came over to notify Isaac and his group that there were some kosher refreshments, which they partook in. Eliezer, however, didn't. But to be fair, he didn't appear to be eating at all. Isaac couldn't blame him. He must have been very nervous.

Isaac and his friends proceeded to one of the dining rooms. They now served proper meals. The groom, bride, their family, and many of the other guests sat at the large dining table. There were so many guests that many people stood, including Isaac, Ariel, Simon, and Thomas. Seeing that their food options were limited to a few snacks, they didn't feel the need to have a seat. People constantly moved around the room. Others entered and exited, going to other rooms where they socialised. Seeing that there wasn't so much space, Isaac thought about doing the same. The noise level was rather high. People seemed to be really enjoying themselves here.

Isaac's stomach rumbled as he looked at the crisps, steak, jacket potato, chips, chicken, and cottage pie served on the table. So many different smells filled the air. He could only imagine what the various flavours tasted like.

Isaac was becoming impatient. The smell of the various dishes was enticing and he couldn't do so much about it. It was all Eliezer's fault that he was here. Then, he remembered Pinchas's advice. He tried to think of something positive about Eliezer.

He looked at Eliezer as he sat next to Mr Blume. He had ordered kosher meals for his parents. Isaac remembered the time that Eliezer called him when he was feeling sick in secondary school. Eliezer always cared about him. He now felt like approaching him to talk to him, but he was involved in conversation with Mr Phillips.

The dining room led to the back doors. Isaac noticed that it was now quite sunny outside. They were all welcome to start making their way outside to sit if they were done with their meals.

Isaac had eaten light snacks whilst talking to his friends. He recited the blessings after eating them. He couldn't help but notice that Simon and Ariel would continue to talk to him as if he hadn't given them the cold shoulder for months, not to mention the way he had behaved towards them. They were so kind-hearted; they were clearly able to overlook his mistreatment towards them and remain friendly and kind towards him. He felt the need to apologise to them. There was a point throughout the meal when Ariel and Thomas were having their own conversation, which Simon didn't pay much attention to, so he seized the opportunity to speak to him privately.

'Simon, I just want to apologise to you for the way I've treated you,' said Isaac.

'What do you mean?'

Isaac felt so much warmth in his heart. He couldn't believe that his friend was so loving that he wouldn't even notice how he had been acting towards him or even expect an apology. He had such great friends.

'I haven't been answering your calls or texts,' Isaac reminded him, and his chest felt tense as he did so.

'Oh, right. I figured you were busy,' said Simon.

'Right,' said Isaac. He figured it would be inappropriate to share with him the negative feelings he had towards him and their reasons. He felt it would be better to simply apologise for the behaviour without explaining the reasons. 'Please forgive me for not responding better. I shall try to do so in the future.'

'That's fine,' said Simon.

Now, Isaac waited for the right moment to apologise to Ariel. He had a feeling that Ariel was a little more affected by his absence, considering his behaviour that day when he showed up suddenly at his house.

Several people had already made their way to the garden to take their seats, which overlooked the beautiful bushes and trees. Isaac, Simon, Ariel, and Thomas still hadn't been able to speak to Eliezer or his parents, though they had managed to speak to Mr and Mrs Phillips upon exiting the drawing room.

Most of the people were still eating and socialising in the dining rooms and kitchen. Seeing that there was so much time left and Simon, Thomas, and Ariel were locked in conversation, Isaac decided to wander around and admire the stately home.

He proceeded from the bright dining room to the dimmer entrance which led back to the drawing room and reception room in the entrance. It was quieter here, which gave Isaac more peace as he joyfully admired the various paintings, photographs, vases, and other decorations in the home.

He ambled around towards the drawing room when he heard the sound of quarrelling.

He peeked into the dark drawing room when he saw the shocking image of Mr and Mrs Blume arguing with Eliezer, who was crouching against the wall – in tears!

Why is the groom crying?! This is not a good thing!

He jerked his head back to be out of sight. He turned around and saw that larger crowds of people were making their way outside to the garden.

That Eliezer was crying and arguing with his parents brought so much sadness and compassion to Isaac's heart, and he thought it was unacceptable that he should be doing so on his wedding day.

The photographer started making his way to the entrance. Isaac waved him away. He then stopped, looking a bit confused. Isaac started moving his hands frantically. The photographer then turned around and awkwardly obeyed his gestures.

Ariel emerged from the kitchen. Isaac beckoned him over. Ariel walked over to him. As he approached, he leant closer to the wall by the opened doors and heard Eliezer being yelled at by his parents.

'Oh no,' uttered Ariel, looking at Isaac concernedly.

'What should we do?' said Isaac.

Isaac then saw a group of three young guys heading in their direction. Isaac's heart started beating faster. We can't let them see Eliezer like this, he thought. It would be embarrassing, and what would others say when they would have heard of this?

'Let's just go in and talk loudly so they can hear us and we shall pretend we don't notice them,' said Isaac.

Ariel nodded. 'Right.'

Thinking that this would be a better idea than to yell at Mr and Mrs Blume to stop, thus causing himself and Ariel to be absorbed into the quarrelling involving the groom's parents, Isaac and Ariel entered the drawing room.

Immediately upon passing through the doorway, Isaac turned his head to the left and yelled to Ariel, who was opposite the direction of where Eliezer and Mr and Mrs Blume were. 'I have to say that I love the views!'

Isaac approached the closest window and felt dumb as he observed the plain street outside in front of the home.

'Yes, absolutely,' said Ariel, going along with the sudden exclamations. He stood awkwardly beside Isaac and observed the plain views that he was observing.

Whatever quarrelling had been going on before had now been reduced to some sniffling.

Isaac and Ariel stood there, not looking back at Eliezer or his parents.

'All right,' said Mr Blume. He cleared his throat. 'We shall see you outside.'

Mrs Blume sighed.

Mr and Mrs Blume left the drawing room without acknowledging Isaac or Ariel, who had suddenly taken pride in the streets of London.

The three young men who had been approaching had actually turned right to enter the kitchen after coming out of the dining room towards the back.

There were long seconds of silence. Isaac and Ariel remained where they were. Both wondered when they could finally talk to their friend. They didn't want to look at him whilst he was still crying because they didn't want him to know that they knew that he was crying.

Eliezer dried his eyes and cleared his throat. He straightened his posture before approaching them.

'Hey,' said Eliezer, now right behind them.

'Eliezer!' exclaimed Isaac and Ariel.

They both embraced him.

'Hey, guys,' he said, unaware of their plan. 'Are you guys enjoying the wedding?'

Eliezer tried to give them a smile.

'We certainly are,' said Isaac.

'Yes, indeed,' said Ariel, 'and we think it's time for you to go outside.'

Eliezer agreed, and the darkness of the room seemed to work well as it helped him pretend to look like he had not just been crying after being admonished for marrying a non-Jew on his wedding day.

The three of them headed through the house and emerged from the home.

Simon and Thomas had saved two seats for Isaac and Ariel.

Isaac turned to Ariel as they stood outside and whispered so Simon and Thomas couldn't hear. 'I'm sorry for not returning your calls. It was wrong of me. Please forgive me. I shall not do that anymore.'

Ariel stared ahead stoically. He was silent for a while. 'You're not angry with me?'

'No, I'm not.'

'Oh, OK.' Then, he looked at Isaac and said, smiling, 'I forgive you.'

'Thank you,' said Isaac, smiling back.

The crowd cheered as Eliezer walked down the aisle.

Isaac stood in his place. Tears started running down his face. He knew it wasn't the ideal scenario, what he thought was the ideal scenario, but he wanted his friend to be happy and not feel any pain, because he loved him. It was easier that he was well-blended into the large crowd, which, to his surprise, had been segregated by gender, because his silent crying wouldn't be so obvious as everyone got up on their feet.

Isaac liked to pretend that Eliezer was devoted to Torah. He liked to think that opposite to him stood a Jewish woman, that her face had been covered by a veil, that the civil wedding was a Jewish wedding, that the gazebo was a chuppah.

He liked to imagine that the registrar beside them was a rabbi, that Eliezer had smashed a plate covered in cloth with his foot, that everyone cheering for them as they walked back up the aisle was wishing them 'Mazal tov' as well as

'Congratulations', which Isaac refrained from saying. He just smiled as he watched them go. He knew, of course, that this was not the case, and he had to accept it.

They had dinner in the dining room, where Isaac and his friends were given hot kosher meals for once. They were able to congratulate Eliezer again, though Isaac didn't, and said, 'I'm so happy for you!'

They then proceeded to the hall, where there was mixed dancing and loud music. Although Simon, Ariel, and Thomas demonstrated their skills in the centre of the dance floor, and the groom and bride enjoyed themselves there, too, Isaac preferred to remain in the periphery where there were more refreshments served. He drank from a bottle of water. The day was turning to night. This would be the last part of the wedding. Isaac figured he might as well enjoy himself as now Eliezer and Margaret were married; this was now a reality and there was nothing he could do to change that. He enjoyed his conversations with Margaret's relatives, who proved to be quite well-mannered and possess much worldly knowledge. He spoke with her cousin, her uncle, and then with her maternal grandfather, Mr Jones, who was quite polite and soft-spoken. Mr Jones enquired much about Isaac's Judaism, seeing that he was one of the only two people along with Thomas who was wearing a kippah, and mentioned in passing that the bride's grandmother, his wife, had, in fact, been a Hungarian Jew.

CHAPTER XLVI

Isaac remained puzzled throughout the next couple of days. Why would Eliezer have hidden this information if it was the root cause of their conflict? He assumed that Eliezer had been unaware of this. Maybe the bride had been unaware of this. But upon further reflection, he realised that this could have been the best possible outcome and that this marriage was better than any other Isaac would have thought of given the circumstances.

He helped his family clear the household of chametz in preparation for Passover, and they sold the rest. Thomas and Benjamin joined them for the Passover meals, which was absolutely fun.

Rabbi Levy mentioned that he was pleased with Thomas's growth and learning, as well as Isaac's aunt and Isaac's cousins' learning. He said that it would be good to have Thomas go through a year of the Jewish calendar before continuing with the conversion process, which would be after Simchat Torah after Rosh Hashanah, after which point, Thomas would be scheduled to meet with the Jewish court, as well as Isaac's aunt and her children.

Benjamin had plans to go to yeshiva in Israel for a year, maybe longer if he'd enjoy it that much, which he and Isaac thought he would. Isaac was very thrilled about this.

Isaac continued his studies with Daniel over the phone, as well as with Adam, Pinchas, and Mordechai in person.

Isaac was looking forward to having Benjamin be in Israel whilst he studied there to become ordained as a rabbi. He told all his friends about his plans, and he was met by everyone with excitement.

After Passover, which ended on Thursday, there was one day left to prepare for Shabbat, and Thomas and Benjamin joined for those meals, too.

Daniel said that the family was considering visiting in the summer, and if the family didn't, he would still like to see him, which Isaac was happy to hear. He definitely wanted to come for Shavuot.

After Shabbat, Isaac wanted nothing other than to see his old friends. He was happy to have seen them in synagogue services throughout the first two days of Passover, but he wanted to spend quality time with them.

So on Sunday afternoon, which was the fourth day of Chol Hamoed of Passover, he invited Simon, Ariel, and Eliezer over. The rest of his family was out of the house at the time.

Whilst Simon and Ariel were in the living room, Isaac asked Eliezer out in the entrance, 'Did you know that Marge was Jewish?'

'I didn't know at first. She later mentioned that she had a Jewish grandparent. I forgot which one.'

'It's her grandmother. It's her mum's mum. That means Marge is Jewish,' said Isaac.

'Oh.'

Isaac saw that Eliezer's face wasn't so changed by the realisation. He figured it didn't really matter all that much to

Eliezer, but it mattered a lot to him. His friend's children were going to be Jewish.

He, Eliezer, Simon, and Ariel found themselves sitting on the living room sofa as the house was quiet.

'So, how's The Team?' asked Simon, grinning.

'The Team is good,' said Isaac, nodding.

'Are you excited to go to Israel?' asked Simon.

'Yes, very,' replied Isaac.

'We're going to have to be calling you Rabbi Abrams soon,' said Ariel, grinning.

Isaac laughed.

'Are you going to miss us?' asked Eliezer.

'Of course,' said Isaac, then looking down, 'but, you know, we've still got many more months to go, and I shall come back to visit. I shall be coming home once I get my ordination to teach here in England.'

'You'd be a great teacher,' said Ariel.

'Yes, you would,' agreed Eliezer.

'You should teach us now,' joked Simon. 'Maybe we can learn something together.'

Simon hesitated as he shuffled on the sofa. He seemed to be half-joking and half-suggesting that they should learn something together. Isaac froze. He couldn't tell whether Simon was joking, and even if he weren't, he didn't know whether the others would be willing to study something right now. He felt a certain excitement, but he doubted they'd all want to learn, so he subdued it so as to not be so disappointed.

Eliezer looked a bit confused as Ariel raised his eyebrows.

'Shall we?' asked Ariel, who was open to it.

'Yeah, why not?' said Simon, now waiting to study. 'Let's go! Let's learn something about the laws of Passover.'

Isaac wondered whether he was dreaming.

Simon got up and headed towards the dining table, where he sat and took one of the books lying there that happened to be written about just that. It was a copy of the Gemara tractate on Pesachim. Eliezer seemed a bit indifferent as if it were still a joke. Ariel was a bit confused, looking at Eliezer and Isaac as they remained on the sofa, but headed to the table.

Isaac waited for Eliezer, who looked at the book and said, 'OK,' and then headed to the dining table to join the other two. Simon had come wearing his kippah. Ariel and Eliezer hadn't brought theirs with them. Simon scouted around the room for any spare kippot lying around to give them as Jewish males were required to wear one whilst studying Torah. The three of them sat at the dining table. It was as if God had arranged a study session with them for Isaac.

Isaac couldn't believe what had just happened. Once he registered all that had just occurred, now believing his eyes, he joined his friends who were waiting for him.

ABOUT THE AUTHOR

Joseph Daniel Estevez was born in New York City in 1994. He graduated from The City College of New York in 2018, where he studied music. In 2020, he completed his Orthodox conversion to Judaism. His learning of Torah would have a profound influence on his works. *Isaac Abrams* is his first published novel. For more information, you can visit www.josephestevez.info

Printed in Great Britain
by Amazon